1/06

The Rachel Resistance

MOLLY LEVITE GRIFFIS

Molly Levite Griffis

EAKIN PRESS   Austin, Texas

**Library of Congress Cataloging-in-Publication
Data**

Griffis, Molly Levite.
 The Rachel resistance / Molly Levite Griffis.— 1st ed.
  p. cm.
 Summary: Just after the bombing of Pearl Harbor,
fifth-grader Rachel Dalton becomes convinced that her
small Oklahoma town is harboring traitors and spies.
 ISBN 1-57168-541-3
 1. World War, 1939–1945—Oklahoma—Juvenile fiction. [1. World War, 1939–1945—United States—Fiction.
2. Schools—Fiction. 3. Oklahoma—Fiction.] I. Title
PZ7.G88165 Rac 2001
[Fic]—dc21

       2001023833

FIRST EDITION
Copyright © 2001
By Molly Levite Griffis
Published in the U. S.A.
By Eakin Press
A Division of Sunbelt Media, Inc.
P.O. Drawer 90159
Austin, Texas 78709-0159
email: eakinpub@sig.net
website: www.eakinpress.com
1 2 3 4 5 6 7 8 9
1-57168-541-3 HB
1-57168-553-7 PB

Contents

Don't read this unless you want to turn into a frog!
by Rachel Elizabeth Dalton
(whose initials spell the color of her hair)

Actually, you probably won't turn into a frog whether you read this or not, but I knew if I put "Introduction" or "Foreword" or some other boring word at the top, you wouldn't read it, and this is a very important part of my story. So read on... PLEASE! If you do turn into a frog, I promise to change you back to a kid.

The story of how rotten John Alan Feester made my life miserable happened sixty years ago, way back in the fall of 1941, when the fires of war flaming over Europe were just starting to sift their smoke and ashes over America. Kids like you saw war newsreels at the picture shows (you call them movie theaters) and knew that some people somewhere were fighting and dying, and it all looked pretty awful up there on that screen.

But the places where those people were fighting and dying were just names on maps in geography and history books, and who cared about geography or history anyway? Germany, Italy, Japan, France, England, Poland—those countries were a long way away from the United States of America. Back then, ordinary people didn't have television sets or computers, so the pictures of war weren't shot into kids' living rooms every night. Everybody—kids and parents, too—listened to the radio and let their imaginations do the rest. Those were what your grandparents or great-grandparents call "The Good Old Days."

In 1940 a really cool radio program went on the air. It was a program that kids then liked just as much as kids now like Harry Potter. The program was called "Captain Midnight." It came on after school Monday through Friday and was only fifteen minutes long. Programs like "Captain Midnight" were called "cliffhangers" because that's the way you felt at the end of each one—like you were hanging from a cliff and about to fall off. If you had to miss "The Program," as fans called it, you always got a friend to tell you what happened. Kid life then, like now, could get pretty boring, but radio programs made it more exciting.

Everything we read and heard made us know

that America was probably about to go to war, a really big, really awful war. The characters on "Captain Midnight" continually cautioned us to be on the lookout for enemy spies, possible traitors to our country, or saboteurs who might be planning to blow up something. We all mailed in seals from jars of Ovaltine to Captain Midnight so we could become members of his Secret Squadron, a group dedicated to preserving truth, justice, and The American Way. Secret Squadron members received a Code-O-Graph badge to wear and booklets filled with secret codes and secret signals.

One day in early October of 1941, Captain Midnight discovered plans for an American base in the Hawaiian Islands called Pearl Harbor. The plans were in the desk of a really bad guy called "The Barracuda," who was working for the Japanese. Right then and there the Captain decided that the Japanese might be planning to draw America into the war with an attack on Pearl Harbor. The men who wrote the scripts for the program did not have access to any classified government documents or any leaks from insiders. They just listened to the news like everybody else, read the newspapers, and made some smart guesses.

On December 5, 1941, two days before the real

attack on Pearl Harbor, the fictional Captain Midnight on his fictional radio program left his fictional base for Pearl Harbor, warning us all to "Beware the Rising Sun." Japan is called "The Land of the Rising Sun." When Pearl Harbor was really bombed by the Japanese the following Sunday, the writers of the program were visited by real people from the real United States government who wanted to know where they got their information. We kids knew. We knew the information came straight from Captain Midnight!

My friend Paul, the only kid in the world who likes geography *and* history, and I were charter members of Captain Midnight's Secret Squadron. We had pledged to unmask all the traitors, spies, and saboteurs in our hometown of Apache, Oklahoma—population 1,938.

If you are not a spy, saboteur, or traitor *and* you can keep a secret, I'll let you read my book. If you want to get into just the right mood, rent the movie *A Christmas Story*, the one about the kid whose father wins a lamp shaped like a lady's leg. Remember that one? Well, my book is set in the same day and time. That kid even drank Ovaltine and had a decoder ring! If you liked that movie, you'll like my book, too.

CHAPTER 1
"We interrupt this broadcast..."

The Japanese bombed Pearl Harbor at 11:55 Oklahoma time today, December 7, 1941. And I'm beginning to think that John Alan Feester, president of my fifth-grade class at Theodore Roosevelt Elementary School, might have had something to do with it. When we first heard the news about Pearl Harbor, my best friend Paul and I were not as surprised as most people. After all, we listen to Captain Midnight on the radio every day, so we know more than most kids do about what's going on outside the city limits of Apache, Oklahoma, population 1,938. Captain Midnight has been warning us that the Japanese might be the ones to drag America into the war. He even thought it was going to happen at Pearl Harbor.

"Rachel! Rachel!" Paul yelled at me as he burst through the back door and into our kitchen. He knocked over three chairs and scared Sally Cat so bad she broke Mama's favorite vase when she jumped down from her perch in the kitchen window. "Captain Midnight was right! He said we were gonna have trouble with Japan," Paul said, trying to catch his breath. "Just heard the news on the radio! The Japanese bombed Pearl Harbor today! It was a sneak attack! America's gonna go to war!" He held his side and kept gulping for air.

I started picking up the pieces of the vase and decided to tell Mama that Paul broke it because she'd told me a hundred times not to let Sally sit in that window. She never got mad at Paul. But then I decided that now she probably wouldn't even care. News about a broken vase was nothing compared to news about a war.

I couldn't believe what Paul said was true. "Take a deep breath and tell me exactly what you heard," I demanded. "Both our radios have burned-out tubes! Daddy's gonna get new ones at Carter's on his way home. I'm the only one here. We ate dinner early so

Mama could go help Daddy set type for the newspaper." My daddy's the owner and editor of *The Apache Republican,* our town newspaper. "They dropped real bombs? They're sure it wasn't just some kinda target practice? They're always showin' target practices on the newsreels at the picture show."

"This was the real thing, Rachel. *Real* bombs on *real* people! We're in a *real* war! It just happened an hour or two ago, I guess. The newsmen on every station just keep yelling the same thing over and over again. 'The Japanese have bombed Pearl Harbor! The Japanese have bombed Pearl Harbor! Stay tuned for details!' The Hawaiian Islands are clear out in the ocean, way past California. I looked 'em up in the atlas before I came over, but I knew where to look because Captain Midnight has been talkin' about 'em a lot lately, ya know. Mosta the telephone lines over there are down, and so many people got killed nobody knows what's goin' on!" He picked up a chair and flopped down in it. "American people killed! The announcers all were sayin' the same thing. They were all sayin' that President Roosevelt's gotta do somethin' right now! They say America's gotta declare war on Japan! They say they might be bombin' us next!"

"The Japanese! Captain Midnight said it was

gonna be the Japanese! At the end of the program last Friday he flew off to the Hawaiian Islands, and that's where Pearl Harbor is! How'd he know, Paul?"

"Captain Midnight knows all kinds of secret stuff! That's why he calls us his Secret Squadron."

We sat and stared at each other for a minute. Then I remembered something really important. "The secret code! The message we got last Friday! Do you still have yours? Mine's locked up in my desk so it can't fall into enemy hands." Enemies like John Alan Feester. It seemed to me that he was looking more and more like a traitor or a spy, maybe a saboteur.

Paul dug into his jacket pocket and pulled out a rumpled piece of notebook paper. He flattened it out on the kitchen table and began to read. "Captain Midnight says, 'Beware the Rising Sun!' That was last Friday's secret message!" he yelled, slapping the table with both hands. "Beware the Rising Sun! And Japan is called 'The Land of the Rising Sun!' Captain Midnight knew on Friday what was going to happen on Sunday!"

Paul and I listen to Captain Midnight on the radio every day after school from 4:30 to 4:45. We listen to the radio all the time, but no other program has anything as neat as our Secret Squadron Signal

Sessions and Code-O-Graph badges. Everybody in our fifth-grade class listens to it. Everybody except John Alan Feester, who makes fun of the Secret Squadron. I wrote a long letter to Captain Midnight telling him that if John Alan Feester ever changed his mind and tried to join, they were not to let him in.

Captain Midnight is the bravest, most patriotic pilot who ever lived, and the program is about his adventures. Every day the show ends just as Captain Midnight is trapped in an airplane with a hidden time-bomb, or he's getting burned up in a fire with no one in a hundred miles to save him, or something else really terrible is about to happen. So far, he and his crew always escape, but we're always afraid they won't make it.

Captain Midnight's archenemy is Ivan Shark—a ruthless, wicked man who heads up an international criminal operation. When war broke out in Europe, Shark was on the side of the bad guys as always, and Captain Midnight began to organize all of us in the United States to fight against him and his kind. Our side is dedicated to truth, justice, and The American Way.

The program has lots of other great characters, too, like Shark's beautiful but evil daughter, Fury, who is brilliant and more ruthless than her father.

But my favorite character is Joyce Ryan, the most dependable member of the Secret Squadron, in my opinion. Captain Midnight must think so, too, because he lets her do everything the boys do. Joyce even gets to shoot down enemy planes because she has such great eyesight. I'm sure she doesn't have to wear dumb glasses like I do, but she's still my hero.

When the war got closer and closer to America, Captain Midnight was recruited by a high-ranking person in the government of the United States to form a Secret Squadron pledged to fight un-American activities. They devote all their time and energy to serving our country, and they tell people like us who have joined the Squadron how we, too, can spot traitors, spies, and saboteurs. Traitors, spies, and saboteurs just might be living right here in our own hometown. The Secret Squadron is a very important organization in spite of what John Alan Feester thinks.

Paul and I joined in September. We mailed in seals from jars of Ovaltine, and Captain Midnight himself sent us official Code-O-Graph badges, which allow us to decode messages. All messages are done in code so that we can keep the enemy from being able to read them. An enemy like John Alan Feester. Captain Midnight tells us to be on the lookout at all times for spies or people who might become traitors to our country. Now that I know about the sneak attack on Pearl Harbor, I think we have a really good suspect in John Alan Feester, but I know I'm gonna have a hard time convincing Paul. Paul and I agree that "Captain Midnight" is the best program on the radio, but he doesn't agree with me about how bad John Alan is. Not yet.

The first day I met him, I decided that John Alan Feester was totally and completely rotten, but Paul insists that John Alan has some good in him. I have yet to see it. I wouldn't be at all surprised to discover that he was a spy or a traitor to his country.

"You know what, Paul?" I said, pouring him a glass of milk and reaching for the cookie jar and the Ovaltine. "I think we ought to consider the idea that John Alan Feester might be connected with the bombing of Pearl Harbor. You said they're callin' it a 'sneak attack,' and sneak attacks are John Alan's specialty, you know." I watched out of the corner of my eye very carefully to see Paul's reaction to what I was saying.

"Aw, Rachel," he told me, shaking his head, but not falling over dead like I thought he would. I piled up the cookies on a red Fiesta plate and gave him a little time to mull over the idea while he picked up the chairs he had upended. When he got them all back in place, he sat down, stirred in his Ovaltine, and began to munch on his cookies. I waited for him to continue.

"First of all, John Alan lives in Apache, Oklahoma, which is several thousand miles from the Hawaiian Islands," he began, holding one finger up in the air to emphasize his point. "Second," he held up finger number two, "he is just a ten-year-old kid who can't even drive a car, much less pilot an airplane." He paused to take another bite and swallow more milk. "I need more cookies!" he said, trying to sound like that giant who stomped around saying "Fee, Fi, Foe, Fum!"

Paul and I have been friends a long time, so I know his tricks. He was acting silly so I'd forget what I was talking about, and he could change the subject. This was no laughing matter. Our country was about to go to war, and as members of the Secret Squadron, we were pledged to help defend it against un-American activities.

"If you let a couple of little facts like those fool you, Paul Griggs, you are underestimating John Alan Feester, as usual. And you can get your own cookies. I'm busy thinking about his possible treachery."

Paul gave a big sigh and continued to shake his head and drink his milk. He had a big brown mustache, but I wasn't about to tell him so.

Neither my parents nor Paul pay much attention when I complain about John Alan. He's such a troublemaker that he could turn Little Orphan Annie against her dog Sandy. He could cause trouble between Roy Rogers and his faithful horse Triggcr. He would love nothing better than being in on a sneak attack. He wouldn't care if the sneak attack were on his own fellow citizens.

Every few months the FBI puts out bulletins with pictures and descriptions of the worst criminals in the whole United States. Our postmaster thumbtacks them to the bulletin board next to the window where you buy stamps at the post office. I always look those pictures over very carefully because I am certain that one day I will see John Alan's mug under the title "Public Enemy." That's what they call the worst criminals of all: "Public Enemy." That bank robber "Pretty Boy" Floyd became a "Public Enemy" after he killed that McAlester police officer in the Kansas City Union Station. That's John Alan Feester: a real "Public Enemy."

Billy Joe Simmons would agree with me that John Alan might have been in on the attack on Pearl Harbor. Billy Joe knows firsthand just how rotten John Alan is. On the Wednesday before our Thanksgiving break, poor old Billy Joe had the bad luck to be in the boys' bathroom when somebody ("Public Enemy Number One"—J.A.F.) threw in a whole string of firecrackers, all lit and popping. Boy, was Billy Joe surprised.

"What in the world is that noise?" Miss Cathcart yelled, jumping out of her chair and rushing to the door of our classroom. We could hear the popping echoing off all the tile and cement clear down at the other end of the hall. Our room, 5B, is almost as far as you can get from the bathrooms and still be in the building. Only 6B is farther. We heard it even though everybody but Paul was talking and throwing spit wads and waiting for the bell to ring for our Thanksgiving break. Paul was drawing, as usual.

"Sounds like a Roy Rogers movie to me," Thomas Woods muttered around the enormous bubble he was blowing with his Double Bubble gum. Jim Patterson and Stanley Wright ducked under their desks like we saw people in the movies do in air raids, but Paul went right on with his picture of Pilgrims and Indians peacefully sitting down to dinner together. The drumsticks on the turkey had very colorful feathers even though it was already roasted and on a big blue platter. The Indians all had yellow hair.

When the noise finally stopped, we all clapped and hollered and beat on the tops of our desks. By that time, Miss Cathcart was running down that long hall as fast as she could to see what had happened.

"What's going on here?" we could hear her yelling. "Where are you? Who are you? What are you doing?"

There was nobody anywhere near the bathroom except poor old Billy Joe, who was still inside. "I ain't comin' out!" he hollered back at her. "You can't make me!"

The firecrackers had startled him so bad that he wet his pants. He didn't want to tell the teacher that, so he just waited and hoped she'd go away.

"Billy Joe," she said when she got tired of pacing up and down, "I'm going to count to three, and if you're not out by then, I'm going to get the principal. One... Two..."

Billy Joe slunk out and finally admitted what had happened. Later he told Paul that he had made Miss Cathcart swear on her favorite cat's grave that she would never ever tell anybody about his pants, him being a fifth-grader and all. He was pretty embarrassed.

She didn't tell, either, but she did have to call Billy Joe's mother to bring some dry pants up to school. Mrs. Simmons owns the Curley Q Beauty Shop, and when she got the phone call, she grabbed the pants and rushed right out the door, leaving

Myrtle Thomas with a wet head of hair. The Curley Q is just a block from the school, and the Simmons family lives in the back, so Billy Joe's mama got back to Miss Thomas and her wet hair in less than ten minutes. But, of course, she had to explain why she had left in such a hurry.

By sundown, the entire town knew about Billy Joe and the firecrackers and his wet pants. Apache is a very small town.

"I heard John Alan laugh just before I heard the first firecracker pop," Billy Joe whispered to us on the playground the next Monday as we huddled around him to get his version of the story. "I'd know that laugh anywhere."

"But did you *see* him?" Patsy Gail wanted to know. "What did he have on that day?"

"No," Billy Joe admitted, "can't tell you what he had on. I wuz busy with other things."

"What *kind* of other things?" Patsy Gail wanted to know, but Paul interrupted her.

"Nobody saw John Alan leave our classroom, right?" he challenged.

"Well, no, but that was four whole days ago. Somebody might have seen John Alan and forgotten it by now," Patsy Gail said, just as the bell rang to send us all back into the building.

"You sound like you're on John Alan's side," I accused Paul as we lined up to go in, and I cut in front. "Why're you always taking up for him?"

"Oh, Rachel, I'm not on his side. I'm on *your* side," he replied, biting his lower lip. "But nobody's *all* bad. Not even John Alan Feester."

Then there was the time back in October when somebody ("Public Enemy" J.A.F.) tipped over the outhouse behind the Flying Red Horse filling station, which is right down the street from the school. Mr. Johnson, who owns the Flying Red Horse, was occupying the outhouse at the time. He was as surprised as Billy Joe had been. Mrs. Johnson had to bring the dry pants this time.

Now, nobody likes Mr. Johnson. He throws rocks at any dog that wanders onto his property, even little pups. And he brags to anybody who will listen that he throws so good because he does calisthenics every day the minute he gets out of bed. That's where you jump up and down and slap your hands over your head and stuff like that. Even though he's an old man, forty at least, he's always trying to get the high school boys to arm wrestle him or race him to the end of the block. Besides all that, his station is the only business in town that doesn't fly an American flag on Flag Day or Decoration Day or even the Fourth of

July. So nobody cared very much when his outhouse got pushed over with him in it. Most people thought it was funny.

"Nature'd just called me," Mr. Johnson told the people who gathered around to gawk at the mess. None of them volunteered to help him push the outhouse back up. "I seen a short person in a red shirt prowlin' around the station a few minutes 'fore I went in the privy and locked the door, but I didn't get a look at who done the tippin'. Too bad I didn't have a couple of rocks handy. Coulda taught the scalawag a lesson!"

John Alan was one of a bunch of kids in red shirts that day. But again, nobody could prove anything. And since it was Mr. Johnson, nobody cared.

Now, we never figured out where somebody got firecrackers in November, or how somebody could push over an outhouse which stood way out in the middle of an empty lot without somebody seeing them do it or noticing them running away afterwards. But everybody was pretty sure that John Alan Feester was responsible.

This prompted Shirley Jean to start the rumor that John Alan could mix a magic potion, drink it, and become invisible. Shirley Jean goes to lots of movies and is known for telling whoppers. Nobody believed her big fat lie except William Percy, the only kid in fifth grade who still sucks his thumb, but William Percy will believe anything.

William took his thumb out of his mouth long enough to tell Miss Cathcart the invisible potion story the day after the attack on the outhouse, and she laughed. But it was a nervous kind of laugh, which made some of the kids think that even Miss Cathcart thought John Alan could do magic. Black magic, that is. It seemed pretty obvious to me that somebody as sneaky as he is just might have been involved in the attack on Pearl Harbor.

Anyway, I had to get back to trying to convince Paul.

"After listening to Captain Midnight all this time, I'm certain you're gonna at least consider my suspicions about John Alan," I told Paul as he polished off the last cookie from the jar. "Captain Midnight says there are spies in our country disguised as Americans, and that there are Americans who are willing to become traitors. If John Alan's not a spy, he could be a traitor. He makes a big deal over the fact that he has never once listened to Captain Midnight, and he says the people who do are dumb and silly, so we know he's not patriotic. What do we know about the Feester family, anyway? They moved here in June and nobody we know has been inside their house. That's pretty odd, you'll have to admit. In Apache everybody is in and out of everybody else's houses all the time for one reason or another. How come nobody's ever been in the Feester house?"

"You're right about nobody goin' in there, but that doesn't mean the Feesters are spies or traitors. Maybe it just means Mrs. Feester is a terrible house-keeper who never makes the beds or empties the trash."

"Well, I haven't told you the worst yet. Last Saturday morning when I was on my way down to the newspaper office to help Daddy, I saw someone who looked an awful like John Alan Feester in a black raincoat sneaking down the alley behind Carter's Drug Store. It looked like he had a briefcase in his hand. What if we found out that briefcase was filled with secret Japanese documents and plans?"

"Rachel, John Alan has a yellow slicker just like mine. And where would he get a briefcase, anyway? And if he had one, where would he be taking secret documents if he was going down the alley behind Carter's? The only shop that has a back door between Carter's and the street is... is...." Paul paused and the room got completely and totally quiet.

"...is Sam Sing's Laundry," I finished for him. "And Mr. Sing is Japanese! John Alan was sneaking in the back door of his laundry!"

We sat and stared at each other.

"Sam Sing is a spy for the Japanese, and John Alan Feester is a traitor to the United States of America!" I said in a very soft whisper.

There was another pause, even longer this time, while we stared at each other and then out the kitchen window where Sally Cat had been taking a bath just a few minutes ago. I searched the sky for enemy aircraft.

"No, no! Wait a minute, Rachel. This whole idea is real dumb! We're bein' stupid. All this war news is keepin' us from thinkin' straight. Mr. Sing isn't Japanese, he's Chinese. And anyway, what difference would it make even if he were Japanese? He's an American citizen. Your father wrote a great editorial about Mr. Sing after his naturalization ceremony, remember? Mrs. Wilhite read it to our second-grade class the next day. That was three whole years ago, but I still remember it because she cried when she read it. Until then, I didn't know teachers ever cried."

"Yeah, I remember that, too. And of course you're right. Mr. Sing is one of the nicest people I know," I said, feeling really dumb that I had thought, even for a minute, that he had anything to do with Pearl Harbor. "Mr. Sing's real glad to be an American, too. That's why he always gets picked to play the part of Uncle Sam in the Fourth of July parade. Every year they try to get him to ride on one of the floats because of his crippled leg, but he always walks the whole five blocks carrying that big, heavy flag. Daddy puts a picture of him in his Uncle Sam costume on the front page of the paper. Always says he wishes it could be in color."

"I know," Paul said, looking down at the floor. "He gave my mother a job one time when he really didn't need any extra help. At least that's what she thought, but Daddy was gone and she sure was glad to have the money." He kept looking at the floor. "I wouldn't even be surprised if Mr. Sing listened to 'Captain Midnight,' too. Lots of grownups do, ya know. I read that in the paper not long ago. Mr. Sing's probably lookin' for spies and traitors just like we are."

I got busy trying to fit the pieces of Mama's vase back together so I wouldn't have to look at Paul. The more I thought about it, the worse I felt that I had suspected Mr. Sing of associating with the likes of John Alan Feester. John Alan was sneaky and ornery and capable of doing dastardly deeds. Mr. Sing was not. The telephone interrupted my thoughts.

"Rachel, have you heard about Pearl Harbor?" I heard Daddy's voice on the other end of the line. He sounded really sad and tired.

"Yes, Daddy, Paul came over to tell me. He's still here."

"Well, I need you two to come downtown now, as fast as you can. Some idiot threw a brick through the window of Mr. Sing's laundry, and we've got to help him clean it up. Come down to his laundry right now." He hung up before I could even say good-bye.

"Well," I told Paul as I reached for my coat, "I guess we're not the only stupid people in this town. Somebody threw a brick through Mr. Sing's shop window. Daddy wants us to come help clean it up. Now we've got two people on our Secret Squadron un-American list: John Alan Feester, and whoever threw the brick through Mr. Sing's window.

CHAPTER 2
Sam Sing's Ache Brick

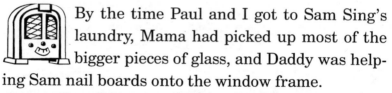 By the time Paul and I got to Sam Sing's laundry, Mama had picked up most of the bigger pieces of glass, and Daddy was helping Sam nail boards onto the window frame.

"Told you this lumber from that old piano crate would come in handy someday, Emily," he was saying to Mama as we walked in. They got that piano before I was born, and the boards had been stacked in the shed in back of Daddy's shop all these years. Daddy never throws away anything, not even the little strip of leather he cuts off of a belt that's too long.

"Woulda hated to have to get Lawrence to open up on a Sunday to sell us some boards," Daddy coutinued. "With all those Barton boys in the service, you know their whole family's all huddled around the radio."

When they finished hammering, Sam Sing sat down in the shop's only chair and stared at the piece of brick that had shattered his window. His shoulders drooped as if the glass were not the only thing that brick had broken. It was a red brick, the kind with the name of the town where it's made stamped on the top. This one was from Sequoyah, which is just ten miles north of us. Most people around here get their brick there, so they're all over the place—in buildings, sidewalks, and brick piles. The piece he was holding read "Sequo."

"While you're cleanin' up, see if you can find the other piece of that brick," Daddy told us. "Put on those gloves I got out of the trunk and watch where you step. Don't want you to get cut. I'm thinkin' the other piece, the one with 'yah' on it, ought to be in this mess somewhere. Might be some kinda clue to who threw it." Daddy seemed to be talking to himself now. "Crazy nut! Can't imagine what he had in mind!"

"I not Japanese," Mr. Sing kept saying over and over again as he looked at the brick. "I Amelican. I took oath. I got papels."

Paul and I tried not to look at each other or at

Mr. Sing either. All of us wanted to give him his privacy, but it was pretty hard in that tiny little shop.

"How'd you know that one half wasn't all he threw?" Paul asked as we began to carefully sift through the rubble on the ledge back of the window. Mr. Sing kept the laundry that was ready to be picked up there. Each bundle was neatly wrapped in white butcher paper, but because of the shattered glass, the area looked like a trash barrel had been upended on it.

"Well, it looks like a fresh break in the brick. Can tell by the edges. Plus there were lots of little red shards around where it landed on the floor. I'm beginnin' to wonder if whoever threw it might have reached in after the glass shattered and took the 'yah' piece back, although I can't imagine what he'd want with it. Just more evidence against him. Little-town police like ours don't have fingerprint kits. The 'Sequo' piece ended up on the floor back of the ledge, so it woulda been hard to retrieve it ... woulda had to climb in over all that glass. He was probably scared of gettin' caught, even though there wasn't a living soul on Main Street when it happened. Everybody in town's glued to radios right now. We were too far down the street to hear the glass break, but when we drove past coming home, your mom spotted the hole. We went straight to Sam's house and then called you."

Mr. Sing did not want to call Joe Moran, the town's only policeman, so Daddy didn't insist. With the five of us doing the clean-up, it only took about an hour, but we never did find the "yah" brick. Mama asked Mr. Sing to come have supper with us, but he said he just wanted to walk home and be by himself. She started to beg him, but Daddy shook his head at her, so she stopped. The four of us watched as Sam limped off down the street toward his house. I can't remember when I've felt so awful.

Daddy patted Paul on the head. "Thanks for helping out, Paul. We'll drop you off at your house. Know your Mama always fixes you pancakes and sausage for Sunday dinner. She sure needs you tonight, son, you bein' the man of the house these days."

Paul just shook his head, and I knew he was wondering for the one-hundredth time where his wandering father was tonight.

"You know," Daddy went on as he started up the car, "we've got the kind of mystery and intrigue you all hear on Captain Midnight every day. You say he's big on stopping un-American activities. The person who threw that brick sure didn't know much about how to treat a fellow American. What's more, he didn't even know the difference between Chinese and Japanese. Not that he should have thrown the brick if Mr. Sing was Japanese, but he ought to get his countries straight, don't you think?"

"Oh, David," Mama said to Daddy, "I'm sure it was just somebody reacting before he thought. I'm sure nothing like that will happen again."

"Don't know, Emily. According to the radio today, everybody in the United States wants revenge, and they want it quick! I remember in World War I how some so-called patriots burned German newspaper offices in several little towns right here in Oklahoma. There was even one little burg in Kingfisher County that changed their *name* because of the war! Went from Kiel, a German name, to Loyal. Takes some pretty strong feeling to cause folks to change the name of their town. Here we are, Paul. See you tomorrow."

Paul got out, closed the door as softly as he could, and ran up his front steps. Daddy headed the car toward our house.

"I tried to get Mr. Sing to let me bring the 'Sequo' half with me so I could take a picture to go with my editorial, but for some reason he didn't want me to, so I didn't insist. When I looked at that brick, I

24

was reminded of something I hadn't thought of in forty-five years."

I leaned over the front seat so I could hear better. I really like it when Daddy talks about when he was little, especially if he tells about being bad.

"When Apache still had our own brick factory," he went on, "Johnny Picket, a kid I palled around with, figured out that if you broke an Apache brick right after the 'p', what you had left spelled 'ache,' like in earache or heartache. The two of us spent one whole Saturday bustin' up bricks 'til we got two perfect 'ache' specimens. Then we scrounged up a couple of red hearts from my sister Virginia's old Valentines. That night we left a heart and an 'ache' brick on the doorstep of the two girls we had taken a shine to. When my dad found all those busted up bricks, he gave me an 'ache' of my own." He smiled at me in the rear-view mirror.

"And you know what, Punkin? Those girls never did figure it out! Wanted to know why we gave 'em used Valentines and busted bricks." He paused and shook his head. "Kinda glad that brick today said 'Sequo.' Poor old Mr. Sing doesn't need any more 'ache' then he already has. Let's go put the tubes in the radio, and see if there's any news about the battleship USS *Oklahoma*. It was supposed to be in Pearl Harbor."

"You mean they might have sunk a ship named after our state? Oh, Daddy! That makes it even worse than ever! Were all the sailors on it from Oklahoma?"

"No, Punkin, that's not the way the navy does things. The men on the *Oklahoma* are from all over the United States. That ship's been floating around for quite a while. It was one of the escort vessels for the ship that brought President Woodrow Wilson back from the Paris peace conference in World War I. I have a feeling it's going to be a long time before we find out for sure what happened to it or any of the other ships over there."

None of us said anything on the way from the garage to the house. Daddy opened the door for Mama and me, but he didn't say something funny like he usually did, something like "After you, dear Alphonse," which was some kind of vaudeville joke about two Frenchmen who never went anywhere because they were so polite neither one wanted to go first. That always made Mama laugh, but nobody was laughing now.

"Well," Daddy said, "I guess I better get these tubes in the radio. That's the only way we'll find out what's happening over there." He put his arms around Mama, and she started to cry. "Afraid we've been trying to put off thinking about it ... worrying about Sam Sing's window because that was something we could do something about ... something we could fix. Afraid it's going to take a lot of time and lots of lives to fix the rest of the world."

"Oh, David," Mama said, "I hope you're wrong! For the first time in my life, I really *really* hope you're wrong."

CHAPTER 3
"Sweet Land of Liberty"

As I walked to school the morning after Pearl Harbor, I had the strangest feeling that the whole world had changed overnight. The streets were almost deserted, and the few cars that went by seemed to be crawling along through heavy mud, although the streets were dry and clear. The kids who were walking to school didn't holler at each other like they usually did. They all trudged along with their heads down as if there were news about Pearl Harbor chalked on the sidewalk under the dry dead leaves and they were trying to read it. But the sidewalks were bare. Even though it wasn't very cold, I put my book satchel down and retied my head scarf real tight on my head and pulled my coat close around me.

American flags were flying from almost every house I passed. It looked just like the Fourth of July. But it was December 8. Nobody had ever flown flags on December 8 before. The wind tugged at the corners of the cloth and made the red and white stripes ripple, but there wasn't any sound. It was eerie.

I started jumping the cracks in the sidewalk to take my mind off all those flags and the war and Mr. Sing's broken window. I was sorry he hadn't come home with us last night. He's a bachelor and the only Oriental person in Apache, so I know he must be lonely sometimes.

"Step on a crack, break your mother's back!" I chanted over and over again. My big brother, Al, taught me that silly rhyme when I was a little kid in first grade. Then the whole next year I drove him crazy jumping the cracks and saying it whenever we walked anywhere together.

"If you don't stop saying that nutty poem, I'm never going to let you walk with me again!" he would threaten. But I knew he was bluffing. He's the only big brother I know who lets his little sister tag along sometimes. I love Al better than anybody in the whole world, even my mother and father. I wondered if Mr. Sing had a brother. Or a mother and father. If so, I bet he hadn't seen them in a long, long time.

My parents listened to the radio most of the night last night, and every time the announcer said the word "war," which was pretty often, my mother would begin to cry again. She tried to call my Grandma West all evening, but all the circuits were busy because everybody was trying to call everybody else. Mama has one brother in the army and another in the navy, so she and my grandma have a lot to worry about.

Al kept pacing back and forth between his room and the kitchen, and every time he walked past Mama she gave him the saddest smile I had ever seen. He would start to say something and then change his mind. He did that about ten times, and then finally went into his room and closed the door. He was still in there when I went up to bed.

When he left, Mama started to cry again. I went over and sat down beside her on the couch. I felt like I was the mama, and she was the kid. "Al's just a junior in high school," I told her, patting her hand. "Don't know why you're worried about him. All this trouble will be over by the time he graduates... won't it?" She squeezed my hand and didn't reply. Daddy walked over and patted both of us on the shoulder, but he didn't say anything either. They just kept listening to the radio even though the announcers hadn't said anything new for a long time. There was nothing about the USS *Oklahoma*.

Daddy hadn't said a word about Mr. Sing's window since we got home. I knew he was writing his editorial in his head. He says he has to put a tight lid on his mouth so he can bake his ideas before he writes 'em down. "If I talk about what I'm thinking, I lose all the steam in the talking," he's told me lots of times. "Gotta go straight from my head and heart to the paper."

I bet he puts his editorial in a big black box right in the middle of the front page of his paper. That's what he does with important editorials, and this was going to be one of those. "Can't imagine what kind of person would do such a thing," I heard him say as I started up the stairs to my room. I sat down on the top step to eavesdrop. "Somebody so uninformed he didn't know Japan from China. It's awful to think that somebody in our little town would turn on one of our own citizens. America'll lose this war before we even get going good if we start turnin' neighbor against neighbor. Sam says he wants me to help him letter a big sign that says 'I'm Chinese' for him to hang in his window. That's sad. Really sad. The whole world's gone crazy."

"Oh, I'm sure it won't happen again," Mama told him. "Somebody just flew off the handle and acted in the heat of the moment. Feelings like that will go away pretty quickly, I'm sure."

"Sam didn't seem to want to prosecute, though, and I can't say that I blame him. Still, I'd like to see the person who did it brought to justice, at least have to pay for Sam's window. But I'm hopin' my editorial will take care of that. Gonna announce a drive to get money to replace it."

I heard him switch the radio off, so I scooted to my room before they caught me.

I know that there is a war going on, and we are in it now. And I know that war is really bad, but now that we got Mr. Sing's glass cleaned up, I don't see how it has much to do with me or my family. Al is too young to go to war. Daddy is too old to go to war. He was forty-five when I was born, so he's old enough to be a grandpa. I'm pretty sure grandpas don't have to fight. And Mama and I are girls, and girls don't ever have to go to war. At least I don't think they do. It'll all be over with pretty quick anyway, I bet. Captain Midnight and the Secret Squadron will see to that.

The only real problem in my life is still John Alan Feester. If he is a traitor or a spy and Paul and I can prove it, maybe we can get John Alan deported. We see newsreels at the picture show all the time about people getting deported for one reason or another. Getting John Alan deported would solve my problems. And besides that, thinking about him keeps me from having to think about all those flags and the war and Sam Sing's broken window and the USS *Oklahoma*.

CHAPTER 4
Benedict Arnold Feester

As I turned the corner and stepped onto the schoolyard, I saw Mr. Snow, our janitor, making his way across the playground, the folded flag tucked neatly under his arm. He's pretty old, so it takes quite a while for his gnarled fingers to get all the hooks into the right holes. He pulled the rope hand over hand—real slow—and we both watched as the rings bumped their way up the tall silver pole to the top. The Oklahoma wind caught the corner and unfurled the whole thing quick as the snap of two fingers. I tried to swallow the knot I could feel in my throat.

Then Mr. Snow did something very surprising. He took off his old brown stocking cap and tucked it under his left arm. He pulled himself up very straight, threw his shoulders back, looked up at the flag, and saluted. I had watched him raise that flag a hundred times, but I had never seen him salute. He held his ridged fingers next to his eyebrow a very long time, and then I saw his lips moving and realized that he was saying the Pledge of Allegiance. The knot in my throat got bigger, and another one came in my stomach.

Mr. Snow is a really nice old man, but he's had a "heavy load to tote" as my Granddad Dalton used to say about people who had more than their share of troubles. Mr. Snow's only son and his daughter-in-law got killed in a car wreck way back when I was in the first grade, leaving four little boys for Mr. and Mrs. Snow to raise. Those boys were all older than me, but I knew about them because Daddy headed up a drive to raise money for their parents' funerals. That's how poor they were. The oldest boy, Joe Bob, was my big brother Al's best friend.

Everybody in town called the Snow boys "those pitiful orphans." The only orphan I ever heard of was Annie, and it looked to me like she had a great life, especially once she got to that mansion. But the four Snow orphans didn't live with Daddy Warbucks. They lived with Mr. and Mrs. Snow in a two-bedroom clapboard house. But everybody admired the Snows for keeping the four brothers together.

The kids who were playing hopscotch near the flagpole saw what Mr. Snow was doing, and they stopped their game and saluted, too. Before long, all the kids on the playground had stopped running and yelling and every last one of them, even the little tiny first-graders, saluted or put their hands on their hearts. Some did both. The only sound in the world was the rustling of leaves across that bare, dirt-brown schoolyard.

I dropped my book satchel to the ground, put my hand over my heart, and looked at the flag for a long time. I had goosebumps all over, but not from being cold. It was something a lot more than cold, but I didn't know what. That flag seemed a whole lot more important today than it had last Friday when we were all running and playing under it without even looking up once. I looked back down at Mr. Snow and bit my lip to keep from crying. He looked so sad that I had to turn my head away.

That's when I saw him. Sam Sing. He was standing under the old oak tree on the south corner of the schoolyard watching Mr. Snow. He had one hand clutching his hat, and the other hand pressing his heart. Even biting my lip didn't keep the tears from slipping out as I watched him limp down the street toward his shop. Mr. Snow pulled his cap back down on his head and shuffled back into the building.

When Joe Bob, the oldest grandson of Mr. Snow, left for the army last June, we all went to the bus station to see him off—Daddy, Mama, Al, Paul, Mr. and Mrs. Snow, his three brothers, and me. It was a really hot day, some kind of record for June, Daddy said, but Mrs. Snow had Joe Bob's heavy winter gloves in her hands, and she kept trying to give them to him. He laughed and teased her and said he wouldn't be needing gloves in San Antonio, Texas, but she made him take them anyway. I wondered if he had his gloves on today.

But I didn't want to think about Mr. Snow or the flag or Joe Bob's gloves or Mr. Sing's window. None of those things had anything to do with me. I wanted to think about John Alan Feester.

I had found two people who saw him at Carter's Drug at the time when the brick was thrown, so I ruled him out on that attack. But he was late getting to school today. I watched as Mr. Feester pulled his shiny new blue Buick into the parking slot marked "Supt. of Schools." He opened the door and got out. Alone. Where was John Alan? He always rode to school with his father. Where was he on this Monday morning after Pearl Harbor?

Maybe John Alan had stayed home to make radio contact with the Japanese because they were planning another sneak attack. Was he right this minute sitting in the basement of his house in front of some kind of fancy two-way radio? Did his house even have a basement? The thought that right this minute he might be transmitting some vital information to the enemy sent a chill down my spine and made me huddle closer to the tree. Did Mr. Feester know what John Alan was up to? I decided probably not. He would be just as surprised as everybody else when Paul and I revealed the truth about his traitorous son.

Paul! That was the most important thing I had to do today. I had to persuade Paul to help me. That was not going to be easy.

Just then I saw John Alan round the corner of the gymnasium and head toward the school building. He was looking straight ahead and stomping the ground as he walked. I waited until he got right in front of me to speak.

"What's the matter, John Alan, wouldn't your big important daddy give you a ride this morning? You been doing somethin' bad?"

"I told him I had to go back for my lunch," John

Alan grumbled, "but he wouldn't wait! Said I was always forgettin' somethin'. So I had to walk! Go away, Rachel!" With that, he turned on his heel and walked off instead of going into the building.

That seemed very suspicious. He had started to go in, then thought better of it. Every single morning he looks me up so he can try to start a fight, and I'm the one who walks away. Where was he off to in such a hurry today? Was he on a secret mission? I watched him until he disappeared around the corner of the building.

Just then, Paul walked up.

"What were you and John Alan talking about?" he wanted to know. "You looked like you were having a serious conversation. You get him to confess to anything?" He knelt down on the playground next to where I was standing and drew an oval head in the dust with his finger. Then he put hair and a hat on the head. Paul's a real good artist, and he never stops drawing, even when he doesn't have a pencil or crayons. Our teacher last year called him "the tackiest colorer in the fourth grade," but that's because he hates to color pictures somebody else has drawn so he won't stay in the lines.

"You didn't tell him you thought he had something to do with Pearl Harbor, did you? If you're right... and I'm not sayin' you are it'll only make him try harder to cover his tracks. Don't think it's a good idea to let him know you think he's a Benedict Arnold."

"I never tell John Alan Feester anything," I said, kneeling down to get a better look at his picture, and so the kids around us couldn't hear what we were saying. At least Paul was giving my suspicions some thought! If I was gonna trap John Alan, I had to have Paul's help. So I needed to keep him talking. "What's a Benedict Arnold?"

"You don't know about Benedict Arnold?" Paul asked in amazement as he put a noose around the neck of the man he had just drawn. He was using a stick now instead of his finger. He added a tree for the rope to dangle from. "Benedict Arnold was only the most sneaky human being who ever lived!"

"Sounds like he might have been kin to John Alan. Was his middle name Feester?" I said, trying to warm Paul up to my traitor theory a little bit more by being funny. That's what he always did to me. "Benedict Feester Arnold. Was that his full name?"

"This is a true story, Rachel. Listen and you'll learn something."

"I'm listening, Professor Griggs," I told him,

pulling my glasses down on my nose and looking at him over the rims. "Continue your lecture."

He frowned at me, but he went on drawing and talking. "Benedict Arnold was a very famous general in the American army during the Revolutionary War. George Washington himself made him a general. But old Benedict wasn't a *real* patriot. He was only interested in money, and he didn't care which side it came from."

"Sounds like Ivan Shark. Captain Midnight says Shark will spy for anybody that'll pay him."

"Yea, Benedict Arnold was *exactly* like Ivan Shark," Paul said as he put the hat of a Revolutionary War soldier on the man in his picture. "General Arnold of the American army, a real rat if there ever was one, made a deal with the British. If they'd give him a whole bunch of money and a high rank in the British army, he promised to let the British walk in and capture West Point without a fight. That was the fort he was commanding for the Americans." He traced a big "B.A." under the man who was now hanging from the tree in his dust-drawn portrait. "He was one dirty traitor," Paul said, smiling at his own joke.

"West Point? That's a military school. Al says he thinks he wants to go to college there. I'll bet Al doesn't know about this Benedict Arnold person. Al would never go to a traitor's college."

"This was a long time ago, Rachel, during the Revolutionary War, remember? West Point was an army post back then."

"Well, it sounds like George Washington was pretty easy to fool, just like some people I know," I added, looking straight at Paul.

"He didn't have any way of knowin' Benedict Arnold was bad. But then Major André, the spy who was helping Benedict, got caught and hung, so Benedict had to run away and join the British army. By that time, even the British didn't want 'im. Everybody hates traitors. Now when somebody turns on his friends or his country, people call him a 'Benedict Arnold!'"

"I don't think I want John Alan Feester to get hung," I told him after thinking it over for a minute. "Deported to another country maybe, but not hung. What was the name of the guy that got hung?"

"Major John André, but he wasn't a traitor to his country. He was British to begin with. He got hung for spyin' on America. They hang spies."

By that time there were lots of kids running around the playground, so I whispered, "Listen to me, Paul Griggs. If all that stuff you told me about

Benedict Arnold is true, how come you won't believe that somebody bad as John Alan might be a traitor, too? And there might be other people around here helping him. Captain Midnight says there's usually a whole nest of spies, not just one."

"Well," he said, frowning at his picture, "I hadn't thought about it like that, but I don't see how..." I could tell that he was weakening a little.

"You just said that Benedict Arnold fooled even George Washington, the father of our country, who, as we all know, was a very smart man. Then why couldn't John Alan Feester fool the people in Apache, Oklahoma?"

Paul stood up and slowly rubbed out the dust-drawn traitor with the toe of his shoe. He took a step backwards and squinted his eyes at me.

"Doesn't Captain Midnight tell us that it's up to the Secret Squadron to fight to preserve and protect The American Way from spies and traitors?" I pressed on. "He says that every week, doesn't he? I repeat, if somebody as smart as George Washington could be made to think that Benedict Arnold was a patriot when he was really a traitor, why couldn't John Alan fool us? I've decided that he's a traitor rather than a spy. I think most spies have foreign accents, don't you? But not if they are American spies, of course. *American* spies talk like we do. In fact, we could be spies with no accents, and nobody would be suspicious of us!"

Paul nodded and chewed on his lower lip. "I guess we could. And while we're at it, maybe we could find out who threw the brick through Mr. Sing's window. If we're gonna spy, we might as well round up all the un-American people in town."

"You're right! We could make a whole list of possibilities! The person who threw the brick through Mr. Sing's window is certainly un-American, and that's what Captain Midnight says we are looking for! We can have a 'Public Enemy' list just like the FBI puts up at the post office, except we'll call ours 'Possible Traitors.' John Alan Feester will be Possible Traitor Number One, of course, but we can have other people on our list, too."

"Why does John Alan have to be Number One? The guy who threw the brick should be Number One because we *know* he's guilty of doing something bad. With John Alan we're just guessing."

"There you go again! We are not just *guessing,* Paul. John Alan is guilty as sin! Think back on how he took over our class the very first day of school, how he bullied Miss Cathcart into doing anything he wanted by pointing out over and over that his father was her boss. A traitor'd act like that. A traitor'd get himself put in charge right away. You just said that's what Benedict Arnold did—got himself appointed a general. John Alan did the same thing. He just made himself class president instead of a general. Same difference. You remember that day as well as I do!"

I closed my eyes and that whole awful Monday in August when John Alan stomped into our lives rolled right before me in living color. It was the first day of fifth grade, and the kind of day milk would spoil on the way home from the store because it was so hot. But the misery of being hot was nothing compared to the misery John Alan Feester was about to hand out to every kid at Theodore Roosevelt Elementary School. Me most of all...

CHAPTER 5
The Feester Invasion

Paul and I got to school early that first day so we could get good desks. The teacher always lets everybody sit where they want to for the first week or two until she figures out who is going to talk to each other. Then she makes a seating chart and puts everybody between two people they hate. So those first few days are the only good ones, as far as seats are concerned.

Besides that, the eye doctor told my mom that I needed to be on the front row even if I have my glasses on, that's how bad my eyes are. My mother had threatened to come to school to make sure I was sitting on the front row and wearing my glasses if I didn't promise to do both. I sure didn't want my mother coming to school, so I did what I was told.

The seat I picked was right between the door and the window, so I could feel what little breeze there was in August. Even if it's 110 degrees in the shade, we start school in August because we let out two weeks in September for cotton picking. Half the kids in our school have folks who raise cotton.

Paul sat down next to me and started drawing and coloring a black stallion racing across a big, green meadow. That horse looked so real, I expected him to whinny.

I slid into my desk and took a deep breath. The hot summer air went through my nose into my lungs and clear down into my new pink, green, and yellow sandals. My nose is not very big and it kind of turns up at the end and it's covered with freckles, but it works great. It fact, Daddy says I see the world through my nose since my eyes are so bad.

I closed my eyes and let the smell of chalk dust mix with the starchy smell of my dress and the wax on the floor and some roses outside the window. It was delicious air, even if it was hot. I took another deep breath.

"You got nose trouble, Red?" a jeering voice smashed into my eardrums.

My eyes popped open. There, in front of my desk, stood a boy with stringy brown hair and beady little eyes. He had on brown Sunday school pants instead of Levi's or overalls, and his white shirt was tucked in. He even had on a belt. His hands were propped on his hips.

What kind of kid would come to school dressed like that? And how dare he interrupt my sniffing? What's more, there is only one person in the world who can call me "Red," and that is my big brother, Al, whose hair is even redder than mine. It's a family curse. But since I found out that Captain Midnight's hair is red, too, or at least it was before it turned gray, I don't mind quite as much.

"I *said*, 'Have you got nose trouble?'" he repeated. "I am not sitting next to a nose picker." He shook his little finger as if he were trying to get a booger off, flicked his nail with his thumb, and laughed very loud at his own stupid little joke.

I, who am often called "Motor Mouth" by even my good friends, was totally speechless. In all my ten years of living I had never had anybody talk to me like that. I am sure that my face turned the color of a Coke sign because it always does when I get mad. And right at that moment I was so mad that my nose began to itch. But I didn't dare scratch it.

Who was this stringy-haired person? I had lived in Apache, Oklahoma, population 1,938, my entire life and knew the name of every kid and dog in town, but I had never laid eyes on this creature.

"Listen, Buster Brown," I said when I finally got my tongue working, "your dog Tige is looking for you." He did look and sound a little bit like that kid with the silly hat in the Buster Brown shoe ads on the radio and in the magazines. Paul loves to imitate Buster Brown: "That's my dog Tige! He lives in a shoe! I'm Buster Brown! Look for me in there, too!" My retort was not too witty, I'll admit, but I was busy trying to figure out who this new kid was and why he was picking on me. We don't get new kids in our class very often.

The big-mouthed stranger stood there with his legs spread apart and his arms crossed just like the Jolly Green Giant. He didn't budge.

I lifted the top of my desk to block my view of him. *If I ignore him, maybe he'll go away*, I decided. It was the first of many times I was to misjudge John Alan Feester. He never goes away.

I put my book bag on the seat next to me and began to move the contents onto my lap as I sneaked a look at Paul. He was so absorbed in his picture that he hadn't heard a word. I raised my eyes, but not my head. The stringy brown hair still showed over the top of my desk like a shock of hay the wind had been talking to.

I stomped my foot in the Secret Squadron signal code to get Paul's attention, but he went right on coloring. Some best friend. Our fourth-grade teacher, Mrs. Keys, was right. He *was* a tacky colorer, and as soon as recess came, I was going to tell him so. There I was, being viciously attacked by a total stranger, and Paul didn't even look up from his paper.

I carefully arranged my blue loose-leaf binder on the left side of the inside of my desk. I sneaked another look up. The hair was still there. I picked up my box of 16 Crayola Crayons and defiantly sniffed them twice before I put them down in the right-hand corner. I put my Big Chief tablet on top of the binder. Then I put my new pencil box right in the middle.

I rubbed my fingers over the smooth, shiny top of my pencil box. It was, without a doubt, the most wonderful thing I had ever owned. The lid was a bright blue ruler that slid out one end to open it. Inside were two erasers with pictures of dogs who had plastic eyes that wiggled. Next was a pair of pointed silver scissors. Then there was a little compartment which held a whole bunch of little gold brads, the kind that fasten notebook paper together. And finally there were four long, bright red pencils with "Rachel" printed on them in shiny gold letters. My grandmother had sent it to me from Corpus Christi, and I was certain that there was not another pencil box like it in the whole world. Now everything was exactly where I wanted it. Except for the stringy-haired stranger. I wished he were on another planet.

I dropped the desktop, and it landed with a loud bang.

The loathsome creature looked at me like Sally Cat does when she's about to pounce.

Just then our teacher, Miss Mae Ella Cathcart, who had just graduated from the college in Durant, sailed into the room, her arms full of books. She spied the bully who was ruining my day and started straight toward him without even putting her books down.

Good, I thought, *she can smell trouble when she sees it coming. She will tell him to find a desk, sit down in it, and stop bothering people.*

Once again, I had underestimated the enemy.

"Ah, John Alan," she cooed. "I see that you found your room without any trouble. What a smart little lad! Do you see a desk you like? Just look them over and take your pick."

"I'm not little, and I'll take this one," the John

Alan person said, pointing to my prize-winning desk with the index finger of his right hand and rubbing his chin with the thumb and finger of his left.

The other kids, who had kept right on talking and laughing and throwing things when Miss Cathcart came in, suddenly got very quiet.

I, Rachel Elizabeth Dalton, King of the Mountain in every game played on Grandma La Grange's cellar, was being challenged for my desk. This was worth getting quiet for.

"Oh," Miss Cathcart murmured. "Oh, I see," she said, when obviously she did not see at all. She hesitated a moment. "I ... I had in mind your choosing an ... unoccupied desk," she stumbled on.

John Alan narrowed his eyes. "But I chose *this* one. It gets the breeze." And he scooted in next to me. I was so surprised at his nerve I slid out the other side as fast as I could move. I stood next to what used to be my desk.

Miss Cathcart looked at me and in a "pretty please with sugar on it" voice said, "You really don't mind, do you, Rachel? John Alan is new in town, and probably a little scared since it's his first day." She had been born and raised in Apache, so she knew every kid in the class. Evidently, she had already met this new kid since she called him by name.

"Who's scared?" he said, giving her a really mean look. "I'm not scared of anything." He turned to look at me. "Or anybody."

Not a kid in that class could believe this was happening. I started to object when Miss Cathcart began to talk again, very rapidly this time.

"Class, I want you all to meet John Alan Feester, *Junior*, the son of our new superintendent of schools, Mr. John Alan Feester, *Senior*." She paused to let the importance of this introduction sink in. This was no ordinary rotten kid. This was a Grade "A" Important Rotten Kid who had a Grade "A" Important Father. Miss Cathcart's boss.

"I know that each one of you will do all you can to make John Alan feel welcome to our town and to our school." She smiled a great big smile, just like the lady in the Pepsodent ad in *Life* magazine.

"You'll wonder where the yellow went, when you brush your teeth with Pepsodent!" Paul sang softly under his breath when he saw that smile. That's the advertising song Pepsodent runs on the radio all the time. I was the only one who could hear him because by this time I had slid in next to him in his desk. But I refused to laugh at his attempt to be funny.

This was not a laughing matter.

As we all watched, Miss Cathcart put her books

down on her desk, and very rapidly opened my desk and took my notebook, pencil box, Big Chief tablet, and crayons and stacked them on the top of a vacant desk in the middle of the second row. My mouth fell open.

Even though she was the teacher, I couldn't let her get away with this.

"The optometrist says I have to sit on the front row," I announced. "Even with my glasses on. I have an astigmatism." My father is big on vocabulary building, and he gives me a new word to learn every day. "Optometrist" was my word for the day I had my eye appointment, and "astigmatism" was my word the day I got my glasses.

"Sure hope astigmatism isn't catchin'," John Alan Smartmouth said, jumping up from my desk and wiping his hands on his fancy dress pants. "Four eyes," he added under his breath so that Miss Cathcart couldn't hear.

Jean Margaret began to giggle hysterically, and I gave her a dirty look. She stopped immediately. Jean Margaret will laugh at anything.

Miss Cathcart seemed to be getting more and more nervous. She bit her lower lip and looked up and down the rows. Her eyes lit up when she came to Paul with me sitting on his seat next to him right on the first row.

"Well," she said with a sigh of relief, "I'm certain that Paul won't mind letting you have his front-row desk. You two have been best friends for years, and Paul is a real gentleman."

We were trapped. She scooped up Paul's books and his horse picture, exchanged them for my things, and turned back to the class, which by this time seemed really impressed with John Alan Feester's power. He sat back down in what had once been my desk and turned his face all the way around the room, smiling broadly at all of us. The Pepsodent smile. He licked his finger and held it up to test the wind direction as he cocked his head in triumph.

Miss Cathcart introduced herself as if we hadn't all known her since we were born. She made pretty good banana splits and root beer floats at the drug store, but she wasn't showing much talent as a teacher. She turned to print her name on the black-board.

And that was when John Alan Feester, son of the superintendent of schools, threw a blackboard eraser and hit the teacher right in the middle of the seat of her navy blue dress.

The rest of us could not believe our eyes.

The first bell had not rung yet, and John Alan

had demanded my desk and gotten it. And now he had thrown an eraser at the teacher!

Miss Cathcart whirled around. She tried to look over her shoulder at her rear end, but since the skirt was straight, she couldn't see the big white chalk dust rectangle on her seat. But she could see the eraser on the floor with the white dust still puffing up in the hot August air around its landing spot.

"Who threw that eraser?" she demanded.

John Alan calmly pointed at me.

"Rachel?" she said in a puzzled voice.

"She did it because you made her move," John Alan said matter-of-factly.

And because his father was her boss and because not one kid in that classroom had the nerve to stand up to this truly rotten kid, Miss Mae Ella Cathcart ordered me to stay in at the very first recess on my first day in the fifth grade.

Everything had happened so fast that I was too stunned to protest. A ten-year-old kid who had gotten his bluff in so quickly silenced not only me but also the other kids who might have come to my defense.

Recess time came, and I stayed in.

But John Alan was not finished with me yet. He

sneaked away from the playground and up to the window of our room.

"Hey, Red," he taunted, "why don't you come out and play and bring your astigmatism with you? You think you're pretty fancy using a big word like *astigmatism,* don't you? I heard how smart you are. Smartest one in class. 'Til I got here! Well," he went on, nonstop, "you and your big vocabulary. I can use bigger words than you can any day. Bigger and better."

"It's not your words that are big, John Alan Feester, *Junior,*" I retorted, "it's your mouth. Your big mouth and your big important daddy."

"Having a father who is your teacher's employer does have definite advantages for me," he paused. "And for my friends."

"Friends? What friends? You just got here!"

"Oh, you'll be surprised," he went on in a sing-song voice. "Many people choose to be your friend when you have influence. It is futile to oppose me, Rachel the Red! Don't be an oppugner." And with that, he turned and ran off.

What had he said? Don't be an "oppuner"? What was that supposed to mean? It sounded like he said "oppuner." He was doing that on purpose, of course, using a word he was sure I had never heard of. I ran up to Miss Cathcart's desk and began to frantically

57

search for a dictionary. I had to hurry or recess would be over, and he'd catch me looking up his fancy word.

I found her big, fat dictionary and flipped to the o's. My mind was racing my finger. "Oppuner... opuner... How would you spell it? I ran my finger up and down each column. There was no such word, I decided. He had made it up! Then I saw it: "oppugner." The *g* was silent. "O pun er," I repeated out loud. But what did it mean? I began to read, "One who oppugns." That's a big help. Back up the page. "Oppugn, v.t. To attack by arguments or the like, not by weapons; to oppose; to resist."

Oppugner. Resister! "Don't be a resister!" John Alan Feester had warned me. That was exactly what I intended to be: Rachel the Oppugner! Rachel the Resister!

At that moment, the bell rang. Recess was over.

I shoved the dictionary back where I got it and raced for my seat. I grabbed a bright yellow sheet out of my package of construction paper, got my red crayon out of the box, and scrawled three words in the middle of the page. I opened John Alan's desk and carefully placed my yellow warning sign on top of his notebook.

When the class marched in a few seconds later, I

was scrunched down in my seat pretending to read my "Weekly Reader."

I was careful not to look up when John Alan opened his desk to get out his pencil. There, staring up at him, were his three words for that day:

Rachel

Resistance   Revenge

CHAPTER 6
Napoleon Bonaparte's Plan

The rest of that morning of the first day of fifth grade would have been really boring if I hadn't been busy plotting my revenge. It was like every other first day of school. Jean Margaret, the giggler, asked to go to the bathroom a jillion times to see how many times she could get the teacher to let her.

"Bet I can go more times than you," I heard her whisper to La Dora. "First-time teachers are easy if you wiggle a lot and beg! They're afraid you'll pee in your pants, and they'll have to clean it up!"

"Hey, Rachel the Resister," Paul whispered to me

when Miss Cathcart started checking out books. He had been peeking when John Alan opened his desk and found my warning. "What ya got in mind? Need a Secret Squadron member to help?" He was trying to make up for the fact he had deserted me when John Alan attacked me yesterday, but he knew I could never stay mad at him very long.

"I'm gonna find his weakness," I whispered back when John Alan swaggered up to Miss Cathcart's desk for his books. "Gotta have a weakness somewhere."

My daddy is a great admirer of Napoleon Bonaparte, who was once the Emperor of France. We have lots of books about his battles, and Daddy has read some of them to me. Napoleon didn't plot out his battles. He just waited for his enemy to make a mistake, to reveal a weakness he could jump on. I would be like Napoleon, I decided. I chose to ignore what happened to poor old Napoleon in his final battle at Waterloo.

When lunchtime came, I discovered John Alan's weakness: FOOD!

"Class," Miss Cathcart announced, "put your pencils and papers away and get your lunch sacks and boxes." Sometimes I walk home to eat, and sometimes I eat at school, but the first week I always take my lunch so I can catch up on what everybody did over the summer. My granddad sells lunchboxes in his general store, so he lets me pick out a new one every year. I always have the best lunchbox in the class. This year I have one with a picture of Roy Rogers on the front and Trigger on the back. The handle's made of rope, and there's a matching Thermos bottle which fits in the lid.

We all raced to the back of the room and grabbed our lunches from the shelves in the cloakroom. Everybody stopped to see my new lunchbox—everybody but John Alan Feester, that is. We all sat back down and began to pull out the usual bologna or peanut butter and jelly sandwiches. Paul, the only town kid who carries a sack, thumped on my desk with one hand and pointed a jelly-smeared finger with the other.

John Alan was walking majestically toward his desk carrying a brown and tan wicker picnic basket. It was as big as the one my family takes on Fourth of July picnics. He placed the basket on the floor next to his desk and opened it like it was the best birthday present ever. The room got very quiet.

We all stopped unwrapping our dried-out sandwiches and peeling our hot oranges and bananas to watch him. He pulled out a white cloth napkin and spread it on his lap.

A cloth napkin. At school.

Then he lifted out a bright yellow metal plate with a red bandana napkin over it. He lifted the napkin to reveal two pieces of crisp fried chicken. Next came a special Thermos bowl with ice around the inner cup to keep the potato salad cold. Then there was a small carton of baked beans. The room began to smell like my Grandma Dalton's kitchen on a warm Sunday afternoon. My nose began to telegraph wild signals to my stomach. I looked down at my dried-out bologna sandwich and my overripe orange. Even in my Roy Rogers lunchbox it looked pretty disgusting.

We all sat there staring like Sally Cat when she's trying to hypnotize a bird. Nobody talked. Nobody laughed. We just sat and stared at Alan Feester's magnificent meal.

For the grand finale, he removed a small yellow plate which held a slice of three-layer chocolate cake with fudge icing. He lifted it out like a magician pulling a rabbit out of his hat. And with the same audience reaction from us. He picked up his yellow Thermos, unscrewed the cup lid, and poured his milk. Chocolate. Then he took out what appeared to be a polished brown stick and pulled it apart. It became a knife and fork. He glanced around the room to be sure he had our undivided attention.

He did.

"What a sumptuous repast," he said, licking his lips slowly. "What a culinary delight."

He started to eat.

Big greedy bites.

His noisy chomping broke the spell, and the rest of us went back to our dried-out peanut butter and grape jelly sandwiches, warm apples and oranges, and half-melted Hershey bars.

I propped my arms on my desk and began to peel my orange as I watched the chicken grease dribble down John Alan's chin. He wiped it off with the bandana napkin, but not before some of it had gotten on his fancy white dress shirt. There was not another kid alive whose mother would put two cloth napkins in his lunch. And if she did, the kid wouldn't use them. There was nobody there to tell him to clean his plate, but he did just that. He was obviously over-weight. So food must be very important to him—probably the most important thing in his life. His weakness!

Therefore, I decided, Rachel the Resister's Revenge would start with food. Or, in the case of John Alan Feester, a lack of it. I could hardly wait until the next day.

CHAPTER 7
The Case of the Missing Lunch Basket

"Come on, Paul," I urged him that second day of school when everybody piled out of the building for ten o'clock recess. "You promised you'd help. We can sneak back inside without anybody missin' us. Teachers don't know who's in which room yet, and with that many kids out there, Miss Cathcart won't notice."

"I'll be lookout," Paul told me. "You grab the lunch basket and start unloading that dictionary box. Good thing we figured out yesterday where to hide it, 'cause we don't have much time."

Paul couldn't resist running to where I was taking the dictionaries off the top of the big box at the back of the room and taking a sniff of that basket.

"Smells like spaghetti with mushrooms and onions," he said in amazement, sniffing around like one of those German shepherd dogs the police use. "And maybe homemade bread slathered with real butter and..." he closed his eyes and sniffed again, "somethin' sweet with apples and cinnamon. *Ummm*. Let's eat it instead of hiding it," he pleaded, rubbing his stomach. "I'm starvin,' Rachel!"

"We can't eat it, dummy! He'll probably go around smellin' everbody's breath trying to figure out who took it," I said, glancing out the window and trying to locate John Alan in the gang of kids on the playground. "Hurry up. We don't have much time. If John Alan catches us, we're in hot spaghetti!"

"It's a good thing this box is half-empty," Paul said, peering inside. "We didn't know that when we picked it yesterday."

"Well, the fact that it's stamped 'Dictionaries' and there's were a bunch of 'em on the top was a big clue, Sherlock," I teased him. I stashed the basket inside, and we piled dictionaries all around it in the unlikely event somebody opened it. It was completely hidden, handle and all. Only the smell gave it away, but that, too, would disappear before long.

Paul closed the box, and I helped arrange the dictionaries back on top just like we had found them. I fanned the air around it with my notebook.

"Nobody, not even starving John Alan, would think to move all that stuff," I said triumphantly. "Sniff around, and see if you smell anything."

Paul sniffed. "Nope, but just in case, I'll open this window all the way. Might make a little breeze."

"We better get back outside. Recess is almost over," I warned him. And we sneaked back outside just as everybody was starting to line up to come back in. We slipped into the back of the line without anybody noticing.

It was the longest morning of my life. I didn't even glance Paul's way because I knew he'd grin and make me laugh, and John Alan would suspect something was going on. After all, I had promised revenge in that note the day before. I knew by the looks Kenneth Stumbling Bear was giving me that Paul had let him in on our secret, but I didn't care because I knew Kenneth wouldn't squeal. Daddy says that Indians are good friends for lots of reasons, one of which is because they are so loyal. Kenneth and Paul are good friends because they are both going to be famous artists some day.

Finally, Miss Cathcart announced that it was

time for lunch. Paul, Kenneth, and I waited for the bomb we knew was going to explode.

We were not disappointed.

"My lunch basket! It's gone! A thief stole my lunch basket!" Frantically, John Alan began to throw books around, open desk tops, even dig in the trashcans. He was like that Wild Man from Borneo in the carnival sideshow last year who stomped Charlie McDaniel's brand new straw hat. Daddy says those people are actors, but I love it. And I loved this act, too.

"I have spaghetti in there," he moaned, "my grandmother's secret recipe sent all the way from Italy! And lettuce and tomato salad and homemade bread and apple pie." Salad! Paul's nose hadn't picked up the salad! That lettuce would really smell bad after a few days in the August heat.

"Now, John Alan," Miss Cathcart soothed, "I am certain we will find your lunch basket. Someone just must have moved it temporarily. Class, let's all help John Alan find his lunch basket. It is brown and tan, you might recall, and it has a nice sturdy handle."

As if any one of us could have forgotten yesterday's noontime performance. We all pretended to look over and under things, but we were all giggling so hard that we didn't put much real effort into the search.

"It's not in here," Kenneth said, feeling around

in the pocket of his shirt. Everybody burst out laughing, but he kept a straight face.

"I can't imagine," Miss Cathcart kept saying over and over. "I just can't imagine what could have happened to something that large." She quickly looked at John Alan to see if he had taken the word "large" as critical of his basket, but he was too busy searching to notice her at all. "I certainly hope your father won't hold me personally responsible," she added, half to herself. But I heard her and so did Paul.

John Alan eyed me suspiciously from time to time, but he never came right out and accused me. He could hardly tell Miss Cathcart that he had thrown the eraser at her the day before and then lied about it.

"Somebody is going to pay," he kept muttering. "Somebody is going to pay for this. I know how to get revenge, too!"

I spent lots of time in the cloakroom, so I could laugh without John Alan seeing me. Since it was hot, there were no coats hanging up there and we had lots of room to hide and peek. When we had exhausted all the places to look (except the big dictionary box), Miss Cathcart called off the search.

"I cannot imagine where your basket is, John

Alan, but I shall continue to look for it at every opportunity. I am sure that your fellow students are very sorry for your loss and will want to share their lunches with you." She turned back to the class. She had a stern frown on her face.

Everybody sat there for a little while. Finally, Kenneth picked up half of his bologna sandwich, tore it in two, and offered the remaining fourth to John Alan, who stared at it in disgust. The bologna didn't tear very straight, and one ragged edge of the bread dangled as mustard dripped on the floor.

"Take it," Kenneth insisted. "It's homemade bologna. My grandmother's secret recipe sent all the way from Anadarko." Again he didn't crack a smile. That's another neat thing about Indians. They are stoic. That was a vocabulary word for me last month. Stoic describes Kenneth perfectly.

John Alan stared at Kenneth a minute, but I guess the hunger pangs were really setting in by that time, because he grabbed the soggy piece of bologna and bread and wolfed it down in one bite. Ruth Ann, the class goody-goody, handed him her banana, but she took a bite first. Jim parted with a fistful of smashed potato chips. Just to keep Miss Cathcart from suspecting me, I tossed him half of my orange, the one that still had that yucky white stuff on it. He looked at it for a long time before he gulped it down. Paul decided to chip in, too, so he forked over two jelly crackers.

"We wouldn't want you to starve right before our very eyes," I told John Alan in a loud whisper. "Might weaken your pitching arm, and the next eraser you throw might miss."

"I wouldn't want you to think you are getting away with this," he whispered back through clenched teeth. "I would report you to my father right now, but I have more interesting ways of taking care of the likes of you. Revenge, indeed. Take a look in your desk, Rachel the Resister."

I lifted my desk top quickly, knowing in my heart what was not going to be there—my beautiful pencil box!

I was right.

It was gone.

While we were all milling around the room searching for the missing lunch basket, John Alan, a Napoleon himself, had found my weakness: my beautiful pencil box with the blue ruler and the erasers with little dogs on them. He had stolen it. I had seen him eyeing it when Miss Cathcart moved my things, and Paul was the only other person I had shown it to.

But if I openly accused him, then Miss Cathcart might put two and two together and come up with four when the basket was found: Paul, the lunch basket, the dictionary box, and me.

I had underestimated the enemy. And I was defeated. For the moment.

Miss Cathcart had slipped out to go to the bathroom, and everybody was yelling and hollering and throwing things. I slammed my desk top down so hard it made a giant pop. The room got deadly quiet.

"This means war, John Alan Feester!" I said in a voice that I hoped sounded like the announcer on "Inner Sanctum," that really scary radio program. "Inner Sanctum" always starts with the sound of a creaking door and a man's low, whispery voice that sends chills up my spine.

"This means war," I repeated. "I, Rachel the Resister, pledge to devote all my time and energy to your defeat. I pledge this in the name of truth and justice and The American Way." They talk a lot about "The American Way" at the picture show these days, especially now that so much of the world is at war.

The other kids seemed pretty impressed that I was declaring war on John Alan Feester, Junior, son of the superintendent of schools, but I noticed that Paul was looking at the floor instead of me. I couldn't figure out why, but before I had time to think it over, Miss Cathcart slipped back into the room.

"Well, students," she said brightly, "I am very proud to see that you can be quiet and well behaved when I need to step out for a moment."

"Miss Cathcart," John Alan said without even raising his hand, "this class needs to have a president."

"A class president?" Miss Cathcart said in a weak voice. "Whatever for? We've never had class officers in the elementary grades."

"To keep people in line," John Alan replied, looking straight at me.

"In line?" Miss Cathcart repeated.

"Yes. There are times, like just now, when you find it necessary to leave the class unattended. I'm not at all sure my father would approve of you doing that." He paused and Miss Cathcart turned very red. "But if we had a class president who was in charge of everything while you were gone, and if that president was me," he went on with a knowing nod, "I see no reason for my father to find out about you leaving the room or the theft of my lunch basket or any trouble you might be having controlling your students. Yes, if I'm the president, my father will get only glowing reports about your abilities as a teacher." He smiled broadly.

Miss Cathcart, who had no doubt been quite concerned about having the son of the superintendent of schools in her class watching her every move, swallowed John Alan's bait "hook, line, and sinker," as Paul's fisherman granddaddy used to say.

"Fine, John Alan, fine. You be the president. Class," she added, quickly changing the subject, "I want you to take these arithmetic papers home to show your parents how well you did today." And she started to hand out the papers we had traded and graded that morning.

"The president will hand out the papers," John Alan informed her. "It will help me learn the names of my constituents."

"Well," Miss Cathcart murmured, "I guess that's a good idea since you are the only new person in the class." She handed over the papers. And our lives.

Right then and there, I knew we were all in for a whole lot of trouble. And I, Rachel the Resister, was going to have to do something about it. John Alan was just like that awful Benito Mussolini or Adolph Hitler. We see them in the newsreels at the picture show every week, but this was the first time we had seen a real dictator in action.

John Alan Feester had declared himself president, and because Miss Cathcart was afraid of his father, she let him get away with it.

And here we are four months later, still being

dictated to by John Alan Feester. Of course he might have had something to do with the bombing of Pearl Harbor! It would be just like him to decide to broaden his territory to include the Hawaiian Islands. I know he likes airplanes. He's always drawing pictures of them all over his notebook. I wouldn't be surprised if he has been taking secret flying lessons.

I can see him now, sneaking aboard a U.S. Army Air Corps plane disguised as a mechanic. He has on a pair of old gray coveralls and is carrying a toolbox in one hand and a fancy, top-secret telephone device which allows him to talk to high officials in the Japanese government in the other. I don't think John Alan is smart enough to learn how to speak Japanese, but he could have a translator. In fact, the translator would probably be somebody living right here in Apache, too. Captain Midnight says they're all around us.

I bet Captain Midnight would be able to trick John Alan into confessing, but he's not here. Paul is. I know I can get Paul to help me. Paul's been my best friend forever.

CHAPTER 8
"...a date which will live in infamy..."

"Yesterday, December 7, 1941, a date which will live in infamy..."

Those were the opening words of President Franklin Delano Roosevelt's speech to Congress today. Miss Cathcart, who liked to entertain us by writing on the board in shorthand, sat at her desk with a secretary's pad writing down every word that the president said while the tears ran down her cheeks.

She and the other teachers at Roosevelt had brought radios to the classrooms so we all could hear the president's speech. She didn't have to call the class to order on this day. The sight of a brown and gold radio on her otherwise empty desk had silenced us all. We had never had a radio in our classroom in our whole lives. We watched as she carefully unwound the long cord and plugged it into the electrical outlet.

While Miss Cathcart switched on the volume knob on the right side, we all stared at that brown wooden box as if it were a movie screen. There was static as she turned the tuning knob on the left, searching for the station. Then the unmistakable voice of Franklin Delano Roosevelt, president of the United States of America, filled our classroom.

Although he used some big words we had never heard before, there was no doubt about what his speech meant. The United States, like the other countries on our side, was in a fight for our very survival. In his final sentence Roosevelt asked the Congress of the United States to declare war on the Japanese Empire for the unprovoked attack on Pearl Harbor.

Instantly we could hear his audience, the members of Congress, cheering and clapping in response to his request. We all turned our heads to look at Miss Cathcart. Even though the tears were still streaming down her cheeks, she put down her pencil and pad and began to clap, too. We joined her and all the other kids in classrooms all over the building who were following their teachers' lead. The noise sounded like thunder rolling up and down the hall of our school. It was strange and wonderful and awful at the same time, and it lasted for several minutes.

When the president's speech was over, Miss Cathcart switched off the radio and sat looking at her notebook for a very long time. We all stared down at our desks and wondered what was going to happen next. Finally, Miss Cathcart stood up and walked to the blackboard and picked up a piece of chalk. She looked at it for a few seconds, and then put it down and went to her prized box of colored chalk. That box was kept for special words or pictures. She selected a bright red piece and printed "...a date which will live in infamy..." in the middle of the fresh, clean blackboard.

"Boys and girls," she said, and we could tell that she was trying very hard to keep her voice steady, "I will start our lesson for today by reading the definition of 'infamy' to you. Listen carefully, please. "

She reached for her big, heavy green *Webster's New American Dictionary*. "Infamy," she read in a hushed tone. "Noun. Public disgrace, loss of reputation, ignominy; an infamous or evil act." She held the opened dictionary to her chest. "An evil act," she repeated. "An evil act. Only time will tell us just how evil. May God help America in the coming days."

She sat down in her chair and bowed her head for a moment. Then she stood up and pulled her shoulders back in a very straight line. "The best way we can support our country is to be knowledgeable about her history," she began. "And to study hard and make good grades so that you all grow up to become good citizens of the United States of America, citizens like Sam Sing." There was a long pause while she looked up and down every row in the room, gazing into the eyes of all twenty-three kids in the class.

"I am sure that each and every one of you is aware of the fact that a truly wicked person, a person with no regard for the property of others, a person who did not care at all for the feelings of another human being, threw a rock through the window of Mr. Sing's laundry yesterday." We all looked down at the floor. "Even though I know that none of you had anything whatsoever to do with that terrible incident, I think it would be very nice if each of you made a point of going by Mr. Sing's shop sometime before Christmas vacation and telling him how sorry you are that it happened. I'd like for you to report back to me when you have done what I asked."

She sat back down at her desk. "We will soon be told what we can do to aid in the war effort, and we shall all do our very best to help our nation remain free. We will start our class with geography today as it is very important that you know the location of the countries, besides our own, of course, which we are fighting for. Open your geography books to the map on page fifty-seven, please."

The rest of that day seemed like it was one hundred years long. Miss Cathcart left the radio on her desk, but she didn't turn it on again.

We did our lessons and waited for the final bell to ring so we could go home and be with our families and listen to the radio some more. I watched John Alan closely to see if he did anything suspicious, but I didn't see anything at all. When the bell rang at 3:30 P.M., we all raced out of the room and headed home without even telling each other good-bye. By this time flags were fluttering in front of almost every house and business in the whole town of Apache. All except the Flying Red Horse filling station.

Because the Hawaiian Islands were so far away, it was taking a long time for the radio news to tell us how bad everything was at Pearl Harbor. Every new hour since Sunday night had brought reports of more and more ships sunk, more and more buildings bombed, and more and more people killed. There was still no news about the USS *Oklahoma*.

Now that President Roosevelt had declared war, it seemed to me that everybody in the whole United States of America was trying to decide what to do next. Everybody, that is, except my big brother, Al. He knew exactly what he wanted to do.

Al wanted to join the army.

CHAPTER 9
"Sorry, wrong number!"

"Join the army!" I heard my mother yelling when I walked in the front door of our house. "Why, Al Dalton! You are just a boy... a young boy! You don't even have to register for the draft for four more years!"

Mama was standing in the middle of the living room, her hands on her hips, her lips trembling. Sally Cat was cowering in the corner, and Jeep, our old bulldog, had taken refuge under the dining room table. In the background, the radio was blaring out the latest news of the war. The people and animals in my house didn't seem to care whether I was home or not, so I just dropped my book satchel on the floor and stood in front of the drawn drapes. Mama must have pulled them when she and Al started fighting because those curtains are always open in the daytime. Mama likes lots of light, but she feels family matters are very private. I couldn't believe she was screaming so loud that the neighbors could hear what she was saying.

"But, Mom! Everybody I know is trying to enlist! It's our patriotic duty!" Al had the pillow Grandma West had brought us from the World's Fair in New York last year in his left hand and was punching it as hard as he could punch with his right fist. Feathers were flying out of all four corners. "Joe Bob has been in for six months already, and he says Mr. Snow is gonna sign for Jack the day he turns seventeen in January."

He slammed the black velvet pillow down on the couch where the inscription "The World of Tomorrow" glowed in bright pink. He stared at it a moment. "There's not going to be any 'world of tomorrow' if we lose this war!" he muttered. "The Snow family is not afraid to do their part to save our country. They are patriotic Americans, which is more than I can say for the Daltons! People'll say we got a yellow streak a mile wide!"

"Well, Mr. Snow has lots of mouths to feed... all those boys around his table... but that's another story!" Mama said in a flat tone. "There will be no signing for early military entry in this house, and that's final! I already have two brothers in this awful mess, and I am certainly not going to add my son to the list! Yellow streak, indeed! The very idea!" With that, she turned and stormed into the kitchen, slamming the door behind her.

We never close that door. Never. My mother doesn't ever slam doors. She hardly ever even raises her voice, even if Daddy tracks mud all over her clean kitchen floor.

I was stunned. I tried not to look at Al. I didn't want him to go to war and get shot at, but I knew that all those things he was saying must be very important to him because I had never ever heard him yell at my mother. I went over and patted Jeep on the head and scratched behind his ears, and he began to wag his tail and whine. I motioned to Sally Cat, but she wouldn't come. Cats never do what you want them to.

When Joe Bob Snow had left for the army in June, we had a big going away party for him. I knew that Al had been writing him letters every week and learning all about what it was like in the army, but I never thought about Al wanting to go to war, too. I was beginning to think that all these changes might affect me after all, even though I am only a kid in the fifth grade.

"Al," I said, sliding down on the divan next to him and patting his hand. "I don't want you to go to war. If you go to war, who'll give me my spelling words every night? Who'll come in my room when the lightning is about to hit my bed? Who will—"

"Well, there's lots more important things in the world than you knowin' how to spell," he interrupted me in a tight, hard voice as he shook my hand off of his. "And lightning never strikes anybody when they're in bed unless they are stupid enough to move their bed to the middle of the backyard, you dumb little girl!" And with that, he ran up the stairs, leaving me alone with the radio blaring out the latest news from Pearl Harbor.

Had the war made everybody crazy? My gentle Mama was banging doors like a maniac. The person I loved most in the whole world was calling me a dumb little girl. Why couldn't we be like we were last week before Pearl Harbor got bombed?

I didn't want to listen to that radio news one more minute. I got up and flipped the off-volume knob so hard it came off in my fingers. I thought I had broken it, but I didn't care. I pushed and pushed it until it finally stayed on. Even with the light on the dial off, that eye in the middle seemed to be watching everything that went on in the room. I thought a long time about poking my finger in that spooky eye, but I didn't.

I curled up in Daddy's big chair and ran my hand over the dark red fuzzy upholstery. Sally Cat's curiosity finally got the better of her, and she crawled over to chase my fingers. She's a yellow and brown tabby and very old in cat years, but she's a great listener. She stretched out on her stomach on the armrest, just like Jeep was doing on the rug, and waited for me to talk to her.

"You don't care about any old war, do you, Sally? You only care about mice and June bugs and not even those much anymore." Sally Cat's real old. She's so old she's lost two teeth, and her eyes are real cloudy. She was old when she followed me home from school when I was in first grade. When Al saw me petting her he said, "Where'd you get that old alley cat?" I thought he said "Sally Cat," so that's what we named her.

I took a deep breath and put my head on the armrest so I could hear her purr. The chair smelled like Daddy, spicy and warm. I wondered what Daddy would think about Al wanting to join the army. The way Daddy'd been acting since Sunday made me kinda think he wished he could join up himself.

I looked at my watch. It was 4:15, almost time for "Captain Midnight." Now Paul and I could find out if the Captain had landed right in the middle of the attack on Pearl Harbor. We were pretty sure he had, since Friday's Secret Code had that warning about the Land of the Rising Sun.

I got out my pencil and notebook out of the end table drawer in case we had another Secret Squadron Signal Session. We didn't usually have them two days in a row, but there'd never been a Monday like this one. Now that we were really at war, surely Captain Midnight would tell us exactly how to go about catching the spies, unmasking the traitors, or spotting the saboteurs.

It was fifteen minutes until the program, so I decided to start my list of "Possible Traitors" in my blue spiral notebook. I'd do it in code just in case the notebook fell into enemy hands. I always tore the Secret Messages out and put them in my locked desk drawer upstairs after I checked to be sure that I had not pushed down with the pencil so hard that a shadow of the message would be indented on the page below it. I've learned tricks like that from detectives in the picture shows.

In Signal Sessions on the program, they give us a different setting for our Code-O-Graphs every time, which makes it much harder for the enemy to break our code, and also a lot harder for me to figure it out. Paul's good with numbers, but I'm not, so he always finishes his decoding way before I do. When I write stuff down on my own, I just use the plain ordinary A is one, B is two, C is three. Otherwise I'd be an old woman before I got through. I printed "Possible Traitor #1, John Alan Feester" using my code. It looked like this:

16-15-19-19-9-2-12-5   20-18-1-9-20-15-18   #A
10-15-8-14   1-12-1-14   6-5-5-19-20-5-18.

It took up two whole lines. Then I skipped three pages and wrote "Possible Traitor #2, Brick Thrower," on page four. It looked like this:

16-15-19-19-9-2-12-5   20-18-1-9-20-15-18   #B
2-18-9-3-11   20-8-18-15-23-5-18.

I hoped the number sign in front of the A and B didn't give the whole thing away, but I didn't have a number or letter for the number sign. I'd have to ask Paul about that. We really needed the names of more people to spy on, especially since we didn't know the name of "Possible Traitor #2, Brick Thrower."

Who else in Apache might be a traitor? Benedict Arnold had Major André. Who was helping John Alan? Who else was sneaky and strange? Old Mrs. Winton who lived at the edge of town and sold eggs was kinda strange. She never said anything to you or looked you in the eye when you gave her the money, just stuck it in her pocket and grunted. That was kind of sneaky. But Mrs. Winton was too old and tired to do all the stuff spies and traitors have to do. I know from personal experience that being a spy takes a lot of energy. Besides that, there was nobody to take care of her chickens when she'd have to go off to secret meetings, so she probably shouldn't be on our list.

Who did we know that had lots of energy and was not patriotic? Of course! Why didn't I think of it before? Mr. Johnson at the Flying Red Horse filling station! He was always doing pushups and skipping rope and stuff like that. Why would an old man like him want to be in such good shape? So he could *run fast* if he was being chased, that's why! Then there was the flag he didn't fly. The day after Pearl Harbor everybody in town who didn't have a flagpole put one up. Daddy wrote an article about how the hardware store sold out of flag holders, so people made their own holders out of everything from tin cans to empty cracker barrels. Some women even sewed their own flags just like Betsy Ross. Everybody in town put up a flag. Except Mr. Johnson. Lots of people were talking about that.

Obviously, Mr. Johnson was an un-American person and a possible traitor. He might even be the person who threw the brick! We knew he had a good throwing arm because of all that exercise and because of all those poor dogs. Paul and I were going to have to get inside that filling station and find some evidence! But getting Paul to sneak into Mr. Johnson's station with me was gonna take an awful lot of talking on my part. I knew from past experiences that I had to start small with Paul and work my way up. That's why I decided to start with John Alan Feester's desk and work my way up to Mr. Johnson's Flying Red Horse filling station.

I turned to page five in my little book and started to write "Possible Traitor #3," and then I stopped. I had to know Mr. Johnson's first name if this was going to be a Secret Squadron official list.

I got the phone book and looked under Johnson. There were about a million of them. Well, a handful, anyway. How was I going to figure out which name was his? Apache's so little we don't even have street signs so there's no addresses in the telephone book like there are in big towns. I could just wander into the Flying Red Horse and casually ask him, but he'd wonder why I wanted to know. Turning to the business pages at the back, I found the phone number for the station. Did I dare call him and ask him what his first name was? I could disguise my voice by putting a handkerchief over the mouthpiece, but what if he asked me why I wanted to know? Besides that, Nelda Jo, our daytime central, would wonder why I was calling a filling station. And if I called from home, she'd know what house the call was coming from. Because of their switchboards, operators knew where every call came from. The numbers were right there in front of them. And they knew where every call went because you had to tell them the number when they said, "Number, please?"

That's the trouble with living in a town as small as Apache. Everybody in town knows everybody else's business, right down to who calls whom on the telephone. At least we have a private telephone line and not a party line like Patsy Gail and Sue. But both of the town telephone operators, Nelda Jo in the daytime and Wilma Jean Perkins at night, are friends of Mama's, and people say Nelda Jo listens in when the day gets boring. What if she told Mama I was calling a filling station? Nope, I couldn't find out Mr. Johnson's first name over the telephone.

I checked my watch again. It was time for Captain Midnight anyway, so I switched on the radio just as Paul ran in the back door to listen with me. We haven't missed a day of listening together since the program started.

I'd just have to wait until tomorrow to find out Mr. Johnson's first name. I sure couldn't mention Mr. Johnson to Paul, not until I'd talked him into sneaking into the Flying Red Horse with me. First, I had to rope him into helping me search John Alan Feester's desk.

CHAPTER 10
Words of Wisdom

It took me two whole days to talk Paul into doing lookout duty while I went through John Alan's desk. I begged and pleaded and threatened to cut off his cookie supply. Even then I thought he was going to back out on me several times. If he knew that I was planning to get him to help me go through Mr. Johnson's station after we had checked out John Alan's desk, he would have really pitched a fit. But lucky for me, Paul doesn't have a crystal ball. He wouldn't have the nerve to use it if he did.

"I don't know about this idea of yours, Rachel," he said, shaking his head. "In order to go through his desk, we have to open the top. That's kind of like 'breaking and entering,' isn't it? I don't want to get involved in anything illegal, Rachel."

"I wish you wouldn't use words like 'breaking and entering.' That sounds like something that happens on one of those detective stories on the radio. I think of it more like sneaking and snooping. Listen, Paul, almost every rotten trick John Alan has pulled has been against some rule or law, but going through desks is different. Don't you remember how Miss Cathcart opened my desk right in front of everybody and took all my stuff out? Teachers go through people's desks all the time looking for missing papers. School desks are public property, and I'm the public. Besides that, it's not like we're gonna steal anything, not like John Alan stole my pencil box. We are just looking for evidence to prove that he is a traitor to his country just like Benedict Arnold."

"You don't know for sure that he took the pencil box," Paul reminded me as he always did when the subject of my pencil box came up. I ignored his remark because I couldn't do what needed to be done without his help. After we got the goods on John Alan, then we could start to look for his connection to Mr. Johnson.

Going through John Alan's school desk was going to be a bit tricky because we had to do it without him knowing about it, of course. We finally decided that the only way for that to happen was for one or both of us to get picked to do the W.O.W.

W.O.W. is the neatest things we do in fifth grade. It almost makes up for having to fill in those two long pages of questions in the "Weekly Reader." Almost, but not quite. I hate the "Weekly Reader."

W.O.W. stands for "Words of Wisdom," and the words come from a big fat book called *Familiar Quotations* by John Bartlett. Every week, the student who behaves best (in Miss Cathcart's opinion) gets to stay after school, clean the blackboards, and select the Words of Wisdom for the next week. Then the person gets to write the quotation on the blackboard and draw a fancy border around it with colored chalk. The next Monday they get to read the Words of Wisdom out loud and tell something about the person who said it. Once in a while there's a tie, and two people get to do it on the same day. We were hoping for a tie.

Getting to do the W.O.W. is a reward for good behavior, and everybody wants to get picked. Especially John Alan Feester, who has a really hard time behaving. He had bullied Miss Cathcart around in every other way, but she wouldn't give in on the W.O.W. The person chosen to do that had to display "exemplary behavior" for an entire week, and John Alan never made it past noon on any given day.

Kenneth had been picked so many times Miss Cathcart finally said she was going to take his name out of the running to give some other kids a chance. When Paul stood up for him and said it wasn't Kenneth's fault he behaved all the time, she made up for it by letting Kenneth draw a new chalk picture every holiday on the blackboard at the back of the room. They were so pretty I hated it when they got erased.

Every week when the W.O.W. is selected, I make a point of staring straight at John Alan Feester while his name is not being called. He tries to act like he doesn't want to be chosen, but we all know better.

"Who cares what some old dead guy had to say anyway," he says every time. But I know who cares. John Alan Feester, that's who. It really makes him mad when I stare at him, so I stare every week. It's kind of a hobby of mine.

To make our plan work, either Paul or I needed to be picked W.O.W. so we would have a reason to be in the room after school. Once we got that far, we would have to trust to luck to help us get rid of Miss Cathcart long enough to search John Alan's desk for evidence. We didn't break a single class rule all week long. We didn't even whisper.

"Paul and Rachel have both shown exemplary behavior," Miss Cathcart said the very next Friday. "You two may share the W.O.W. honor. And since I have a teachers' meeting immediately after school, I am going to count on your good behavior continuing when you are left alone in the room."

As always, I was staring at John Alan when she named Paul and me. John Alan clamped his teeth shut hard and narrowed his eyes. I, Rachel the Resister, had won this week's battle for sure. The 3:30 bell rang.

"Class dismissed," Miss Cathcart sang out about five seconds after everybody had rushed out the door. She has an awful hard time being in charge. "Now don't forget to close the door behind you when you leave," she sang out as she gathered up stacks of papers she was taking home to grade. "Mr. Snow cleans my room last, so he won't get here until about five o'clock. You all should be finished and gone before that."

"Yes, ma'am," I said, trying to control my excitement. We were almost home free! This was even worth missing "Captain Midnight" on a Friday. Friday's shows are always the most exciting ones, and then we have to wait almost three whole days to find out what happened. But this was more important.

97

"Well, I'll see you both on Monday. Behave yourselves," Miss Cathcart admonished us with a big grin. And then she was gone.

I saw Al walking by the window, so I hollered at him to tell Mama I'd be late getting home. Then I headed for John Alan's desk.

"No," Paul stopped me. "We have to do the W.O.W. first."

"Oh, come on, Paul, just a quick peek. Bet ya a dozen Hershey bars with almonds the first thing we find's a map of Hawaii. Might even find my pencil box in there, too! I've never stopped wondering where he keeps it!"

"Oh, he'd never bring *that* back to school," Paul assured me. "Somebody'd see it and tell. You made such a fuss, they all know what it looks like. Besides, you still don't know for *sure* that John Alan took it."

"Oh, he's the thief, all right. Who else could it be?"

I had done everything I could think of to try to get my pencil box back from John Alan in the first few weeks after it disappeared, but Paul finally convinced me that it was hopeless. We had joined the Secret Squadron a couple of weeks after the box was taken, and Paul said I was wasting valuable time looking for it—time that could be better spent looking for spies and traitors and saboteurs. I decided that he was right.

"If he did take it—and I still say *if*—he would keep it hidden some place in his house," Paul assured me. "You can't go breaking into his house, can you? Might as well forget it."

And I had forgotten it. Until now. I started to raise the top of the desk.

"No! We have to let some time go by. Kids always forget stuff and come back. If we're caught, John Alan'll find out about it. People wander in and out for fifteen minutes after school, and you know it. Won't be safe to open that desk until after the buses leave. Come on and help me pick the Words of Wisdom."

He was right, but it was taking all the willpower I had not to rip open the top of John Alan's desk and start rummaging.

"Do you realize that this very desk might contain the plans to invade California?" I whispered, tapping the desk with my pencil. "California! That's the closest state to the Hawaiian Islands. I heard a man on the news last night say it might be the next place to get bombed."

"Then we need to figure out exactly how far California is from Oklahoma," Paul replied, running his finger down the columns of the index in *Familiar Quotations*. "What topic do we want?"

"Something about spies or traitors, of course," I told him.

"No, Rachel, we don't want to tip John Alan off," Paul told me in a voice that reminded me of my father when he gets disgusted with me. "You're not usin' your head. John Alan is not as dumb as you wish he was. You say he's dumb because you don't like him. Actually, he's very smart."

If we had only known that at that very moment, John Alan was crouched outside the window listening to every word we said, I would have known how right Paul was. But we didn't know that until later. Much later.

"At least look under 'treason,'" I insisted. "I want to see if they have any quotes from that Benedict Arnold guy even if we don't use it."

"I doubt that he said anything worth remembering," Paul told me as he turned to the index. "Treason... treason... here it is! The very first one says 'Treason against the United States'!"

"What page? What page is that on?" I wanted to know. "That's exactly what we're lookin' for! John Alan is a traitor who has committed treason!"

"This quote comes straight from the Constitution

of the United States," Paul said, flipping back toward the front of the book. "It's on page 474a."

"The 'a' means it's in the left-hand column," I told him.

"Rachel, I have been the W.O.W. four times, and you have only been it three. I *know* that 'a' means the left-hand column."

Sometimes, Paul can be very irritating. This was one of those times.

"Listen to this!" and he began to read in a voice that sounded like Edward R. Morrow on the radio when he broadcasts from London. " 'Treason against the United States shall consist only in levying war against them, or in adhering to their enemies, giving them aid and comfort.' "

" 'Aid and comfort to the enemy,' " I repeated, looking over his shoulder. "I've heard about that, but I don't think John Alan Feester would give aid or comfort to anybody, enemy or otherwise. Wait! Keep on reading! Here's what we've been looking for. Listen to what it says right here in the Constitution of the United States of America, Paul! It says: 'No person shall be convicted of treason unless on the testimony of two witnesses to the same overt act, or on confession in open court.' Hurrah! That's what I wanted to know!"

"*What's* what you wanted to know?" Paul asked.

"I wanted to know what it took to convict someone of being a traitor, and the Constitution says it only takes two witnesses!" I yelled triumphantly. "That's all it takes to convict somebody of treason! Two witnesses! You and me! I was afraid it would take a lot more than that! John Alan Feester is deported already!" I beat on the desk with both fists. "Now all we have to do is spy on him until the two of us witness him doing something awful, something like signaling enemy aircraft at night with a flashlight or sneaking aboard an American ship with a bomb in a suitcase. We just have to be sure that both of us see him do it because it says we have to have two witnesses. You and me."

"Two witnesses," Paul repeated slowly. "Two witnesses can brand you a traitor," he said, staring out the window at the trees on the playground. He bit his lip as he read again, "'...same overt act...' What does 'overt' mean?"

"Don't know. Let's look it up," I replied, heading for Miss Cathcart's big dictionary. I flipped to the o's. "'Overt... open to view; public; apparent.' Well, we haven't actually *seen* John Alan do anything yet, so we couldn't swear to his treason under oath. Not yet anyway. We can't swear until we actually catch him, but we can do that. I just know we can!"

"We couldn't, but there might be two people who

could," Paul said, still looking out at the trees. "There might already be two people who could swear about the actions of a traitor and get him deported."

"Two people who saw John Alan committing a traitorous act?" I asked him, tugging on his shirtsleeve, trying to get him to look at me instead of out the window. "Who are they? What did they see him do?"

"No, that's not what I mean," Paul said, looking back at me with narrowed eyes. "What do you suppose 'open court' means?"

"Oh, I don't know. That wouldn't be in the dictionary. But what were you saying about two witnesses? What did two people witness John Alan doing, and who were the two people?"

"Hey!" Paul shouted. "Look! It's four o'clock! Time for the search!"

As I dove into John Alan's desk, the subject of two witnesses dove into the deep waters of my mind and didn't surface for a long time.

"Let me check the hall," Paul said, running to the door and looking to the right and left as well as up at the ceiling.

"You think somebody'd be hanging from the transom?" I teased.

"You can't be too careful," he said as he ran back and sat down next to me in John Alan's seat.

"Captain Midnight says traitors are often very close by, and we don't even know it," he said, chewing on his lip again as I opened the desktop. "What a mess. I was going to tell you not to get his stuff out of order, but it looks like a cyclone has been through here. There is no order."

It was true. John Alan's desk was a disaster. Still, we carefully stacked the things from top to bottom so we could put it all back like we found it. We took turns running back and forth to the doors to be sure that nobody would walk in and surprise us, but the building appeared to be deserted.

We could hear Mr. Snow emptying wastebaskets and banging the seats on the desks as he swept the rooms down the hall. As long as those noises went on, we knew we were safe from him, at least.

I was holding my breath and hoping beyond hope that we would find something really incriminating, like plans written in Japanese or photographs of Pearl Harbor taken from an enemy airplane, but we only found broken pencils, erasers, and crumpled-up notebook paper. There were lots of stubby crayons and a smashed Crayola box. A half-eaten Baby Ruth candy bar had melted and made a sticky mess near the bottom of the pile. There was lots of other junk, too. A couple of leaves, two shiny rocks, and a picture of a half-naked lady. Paul spied the half-naked lady before I could get a good look at her, and he stuck the picture behind his back.

"Lemme see what you found!" I demanded. "Lemme see!"

"Nope," Paul said with a wicked grin. "You are too young!"

"Is she Japanese? At least tell me that much! If she's Japanese that would be very incriminating evidence, don't you think?"

Paul looked over his shoulder, almost breaking his neck to get a better view. "No," he said slowly as he studied the woman more closely. "She's not Japanese. In fact, it's signed 'Gypsy Rose Lee,' and her fans cover all the important stuff." He then handed the picture to me so I'd believe him.

"Oh, he got that at the State Fair in Oklahoma City," I said, disgusted at Paul's apparent interest in the picture. "Don't you remember him tellin' about it at recess every day for a month?"

"Yeah," Paul said, getting a dumb look on his face. "The woman he saw wasn't the *real* Gypsy Rose Lee, but she was a good friend of Gypsy Rose Lee's cousin. That's where she got all those pictures to sell. He musta told us a hundred times about the end of her dance when she pulled back all her fans, and all she had on was three Band-Aids." He sighed when he said "three Band-Aids."

"Three Band-Aids! You never told me that before! He never told that in front of the girls! I bet they weren't real Band-Aids. Havin' just three Band-Aids on would make you look like you were almost stark naked. And it would hurt when you took 'em off. No woman in her right mind would dance in front of people with just three Band-Aids on!" I punched him on the arm real hard. "I bet that's not her real autograph either!"

"Well, that woman at the State Fair only had on three Band-Aids," Paul insisted, "and John Alan Feester is the only kid in Apache, Oklahoma, who saw her." He put the picture back in John Alan's desk right on top so he could look at it one last time before he dropped the lid.

I started to point out the utter stupidity of Paul's admiration of John Alan, but I knew it was useless. "That picture was *not* on top," I told him. "He would never have left it right on top. The minute he opened his desk on Monday, John Alan would know somebody had been messing with his stuff. Some spy you'd make." I opened the desk again and stuck Gypsy Rose Lee right where she belonged, in the middle of a mess. "Captain Midnight would expel you from the Secret Squadron for that kind of blunder."

"Well, it is almost time for Mr. Snow to get here, and we haven't found a single piece of incriminating evidence," Paul declared. "And we haven't picked our quote for the W.O.W. either." He picked up the *Familiar Quotations* again. "You do the border, I'll find a quote. Don't like doing borders. Bet I can find something from Benjamin Franklin. I've been reading the almanac Mr. Schwartz at the meat market gave us for Christmas, and it has lots of Ben Franklin quotes. He said lots of smart things. Funny, too. I check his *Poor Richard's Almanac* out from the library all the time."

I began an elaborate border using reds and purples and yellows, but I was still thinking about John Alan so much that I pushed down too hard and snapped the yellow piece in two.

"You better be careful," Paul warned me. "You know how particular Miss Cathcart is about her colored chalk. Hey, Benjamin Franklin must have known John Alan. Listen to this: 'Eat to live and not live to eat.' Want to use that one and watch John Alan's face when he sees it?"

"Nope, it would just remind him of his lost lunch basket, and he would moan about it for the one-thousandth time. Let me look." I started to slide into the desk when I realized my fingers were covered with red, purple, and yellow chalk dust. I almost wiped them on my plaid skirt, but then I remembered not even Oxydol will get chalk dust out.

"Mama'll wring my neck if I get this chalk on my clothes. That stuff's real hard to get out. What'll I do?" I asked Paul, holding up my rainbow fingers. But he was too engrossed in *Familiar Quotations* to hear me.

"I need something to wipe it off on," I said to myself, carefully opening the cupboards that line the wall of our room with my clean left hand. I slid open door after door, looking for an old rag of some kind. Finally, I found an old torn-up undershirt left from an art class and was rubbing my last finger clean when I saw what I had been looking for all along—evidence of treachery! An *Atlas of the World* was lying on the bottom shelf with what looked like a long purple and red streamer of crepe paper sticking out from the top.

"Paul! Look! This may be what we've been looking for!" I shouted, pulling the atlas out and placing it on the closest desk—John Alan's. I let it fall open to the first marked page.

Japan!

Somebody had marked Japan with what I now recognized as a smashed flat Hawaiian lei.

"It's a lei! Just like the ones hula-hula girls wear in the movies! Hawaiian hula-hula girls!" I quickly flipped to the other spot, which also held a smashed lei. I opened it slowly and lifted out the flattened red lei. Below it was a double-page map of the Hawaiian Islands.

Success!

"But Rachel," Paul said, looking over my shoulder, "that doesn't prove anything. So somebody marked two maps with two crepe paper leis. What does that prove?"

"Somebody?" I yelled at him. "Look whose desk is next to the cabinet. John Alan Feester's! Look carefully, because you are one of two witnesses!"

"I hate to tell you this 'cause ya might turn me in to the FBI, but I looked the Hawaiian Islands up in the atlas I checked out at the library. Wanted to see how far they were from California. Looked up Japan, too. To see how far those planes had to fly to get to Pearl Harbor. And before I closed the atlas, I marked both places so I could look at 'em again. Even if you could prove that John Alan marked those pages, that's not enough evidence to get somebody deported. They don't deport people for looking at maps, Rachel. Besides that, there are two other desks very close to that atlas. Jean Margaret's and Patsy Gail's. Miss Cathcart put John Alan in between them so they'd stop whisperin'."

I looked at him for a full ten seconds without saying anything. "I guess you're right," I finally admitted. "But those leis. Leis come from Hawaii, right? They might be evidence, they really might."

"Leis like that also come from the State Fair of Oklahoma, Rachel, and we *know* John Alan went to the State Fair. We don't know that he went to Hawaii. We gotta find something really big...like plans for Pearl Harbor with the spots they bombed marked in red or telegrams of instructions from the Japanese addressed to Mr. John Alan Feester, Junior. Somethin' bigger than maps in an atlas or smashed Hawaiian leis."

I went back to my own seat and sat down. "Proving than John Alan is a traitor is turning out to be a much bigger job than I thought it would be. Maybe we ought to go for spy or saboteur for him. In fact, I bet it would be a lot easier to find out who threw the brick through Mr. Sing's window, don't you?" I needed to plant some seeds for my idea about Mr. Johnson and his filling station. I'd tell Paul the "yah" brick might be in there. Paul was really interested in who threw that brick. He'd said so when we talked about making up our list of Possibles. "Yep, I bet trying to witness John Alan doing something will be harder than finding that brick thrower."

Just then, Mr. Snow walked in.

CHAPTER 11
Mr. Snow's Closet Secret

"What's that about the brick? Did ya say they found out who done it?" Mr. Snow asked as he flipped up the desk seats and sprinkled floor cleaner under each one. It's that wonderful waxy looking stuff that looks like the shavings from a hundred red pencils. My nose started twitching like Sally Cat's when she gets a whiff of catnip. He shook it in a rainbow-shaped pattern across the front of the room as I sniffed and sniffed.

"Nope," I answered, "nobody's found the other half of the brick yet either, the half that says 'yah.' Daddy says Mr. Sing's scared ta get his window fixed, even though Daddy collected more than enough money. He's still afraid whoever threw the first one might not have figured out where Mr. Sing's from. He's still got the window boarded up and that sign that says 'I Am Chinese' on it." I took another deep sniff. "Is it true that you are going to sign for Jack so he can go in the army early? Joe Bob told Al that in a letter last week. Said you'd promised to sign the day Jack turned seventeen. Joe Bob and Al write to each other all the time."

"Yep," Mr. Snow replied, not looking up from his broom. "I reckon there's no use having a fight about it here. He's gonna see fightin' enough before long anyway. If I don't sign now, he'll just go on his own when he's of age." He paused a minute and then looked up at me again. "Sing's not a Jap, you say?"

"Yeah, that's right. He came from China to New York, and then from New York straight here to Oklahoma by train. He told Daddy he picked Oklahoma because he liked what he saw about it in the movies. He really wanted to be a cowboy, but he never could learn to ride a horse."

"Sing wanted to be a cowboy? Had a hankerin' to do that myself," Mr. Snow said with a long, slow smile. "First time I tried to climb on a filly's back I got my genuine leather boot stuck in the stirrup and dang near broke my neck and ankle both tryin' to get it back out." He looked out the window like he was trying to see into the past. "Bet Sing didn't have leather boots."

Mr. Snow looked even older and more tired than usual today, and I couldn't help remembering how straight and tall he stood when he was saying the Pledge of Allegiance the day after Pearl Harbor.

I wished I could make him feel better. "Don't you worry about havin' to sign for Jack, Mr. Snow. This war's not gonna last very long. It'll be over before you have to sign. I just know it will."

"Wish you was right, Missy. Sure do. But that ain't the way wars 'ave gone in the past. They's always over later rather than sooner. 'Fore they're done with thisun, all four 'a my boys'll be in uniform. You wait and see! Dirty rotten Japs! Wish we'd bomb 'em off the face of the earth!" He was sweeping faster and faster as he talked, and finally he smacked the broom hard against the floor, scattering the trash he had just swept up all over the room. He looked up at me again. "You *sure* Sing's a Chinaman 'stead of a Jap?"

"Sure I'm sure," I told him, wondering why he was so interested in Mr. Sing. "Daddy says lots of people think all Orientals come from the same country, just like they think all Indians are from the same tribe. But they're not. Each tribe's as different from the other as Japanese are from Chinese, Daddy says."

Mr. Snow has been our janitor since I started first grade, but I'd never talked to him very much, and I'd sure never seen him mad. He was always calm and peaceful and slow. But when he was knocking that broom around he looked just like Al when he and Mama were fighting over the army, mad one minute and mixed up the next. This war was changing everybody and none of those changes was for the good, it seemed to me.

"Your pa got any idea who throwed that brick?" he asked, beginning to scrape the broom back and forth trying to gather up the mess again.

"Nope, all we know's that it was made in Sequoyah. The piece we found's got 'Sequo' stamped on it. Daddy says if we could find the half with 'yah,' it'd be a clue. We think he took it with him. 'Course, just havin' the brick wouldn't mean the person was guilty. That would just be circumstantial evidence. That was my word for the day yesterday, *circumstantial*, meaning 'incidental or not of great importance.' What we'd need is a motive, Daddy says, a real strong *reason* for doin' it."

Mr. Snow had stopped sweeping and was leaning on his broom and listening to me like I was an announcer giving the latest war news on the radio. Suddenly, he looked away and muttered, "That Miss Cathcart sure likes fresh air, don't she?" as he made his way down the row, slamming shut window after window.

"She says heated air is unhealthy for our lungs," Paul explained, looking up from the *Familiar Quotations,* "so she gives us all pneumonia in order to save our lives. Here's a Ben Franklin quote we can use, Rachel. 'Three may keep a secret if two of them are dead.' Captain Midnight talks about keepin' secrets all the time. In war time, ya gotta keep secrets. 'Three may keep a secret if two of them are dead.' That's pretty funny. Funny but true, especially if one of the three is a girl."

"That's not true! You and I keep secrets all the time. We're probably the best two secret keepers in this whole town. Bet you can keep a secret, too, can't you, Mr. Snow?" I teased, trying to make him smile. "Bet you hear lots of good gossip and read lots of secrets in notes you find when you're sweepin' up, don't ya?"

"My ears ain't what they used to be, Missy, and I got better things to do with my time than read kids' notes. Speakin' of time, yours is 'bout up. I gotta lock up and get home to supper. Mrs. Snow's fixing pork chops and gravy. All four 'a my boys is gonna be at our table at the same time! Be lockin' the doors in five minutes," he said as he headed down the hall toward his janitor's closet.

Paul quickly wrote in my stupendously colorful border: "Three may keep a secret if two of them are dead. B. Franklin." We put on our coats and started to turn off the lights when I spotted a box on the floor next to Miss Cathcart's desk.

"Wait a second, Paul, Mr. Snow forgot his box of floor cleaner. Let's take it to him since he's in a hurry to get home. I'm glad they're getting to all be together. I didn't know Joe Bob was home for Christmas already."

We started down the hallway, which seemed ten times longer and spookier with no kids in it but us. The gray walls looked cold and lonely. We didn't say a word because it was so still and quiet it seemed like we were in church. Mr. Snow's closet door was halfway open, so I took one last sniff of the box, pushed the door open, and stepped in to hand him the cleaner.

The only light inside was a single bare bulb hanging down from the ceiling in the middle of the tiny room. Mr. Snow was standing in front of a makeshift desk he had put together with a board on top of two orange crates. The only thing on his little desk was a framed picture of Mrs. Snow with the four grandsons. It had been taken in a picture studio a long time ago. The boys were all little, and they were laughing and hugging each other and Mrs. Snow. They all looked very happy. Mr. Snow was staring at the picture. The "yah" brick was in his hand. He dropped it when he saw me. It landed with a clunk that echoed in the tiny little room.

"You . . . you forgot your floor cleaner," I told him, handing him the box. Paul was standing right behind me, but neither one of us looked down at the brick on the floor. We all three stood there in that little room, looking at each other for what seemed like an hour. Finally, Paul broke the silence.

"Sure is dark in here, Mr. Snow. Can't hardly see my hand in front of my face, can you, Rachel?"

"Nope, sure can't," I assured them both. "Can't see anything in this room at all. Need to get you a bigger watt bulb, Mr. Snow." I stepped back outside the room. "We're leavin' now. You better be gettin' on home to supper. Don't want those pork chops gettin' cold. You tell Joe Bob to come see us soon, ya hear? Al's been missin' him somethin' awful. We've all been friends for a real long time, haven't we? Really good friends. In fact, we think you're just like family." I ran out of words.

"Thank you," Mr. Snow said softly. "Thank you for not bein' able to see."

Paul and I ran down the hall and out the door and didn't say a word until we got off the playground and onto the sidewalk to my house.

"Do you suppose he thinks we'll tell on him, Paul? I hope he won't worry about that. I'm sure glad I said what I did earlier about us being good secret keepers. I wouldn't want him to worry, would you?"

"No, I wouldn't want him to worry about that."

"I won't tell. Not Daddy or Al or Mama. Not anybody. Mr. Snow's not a mean person, not like John Alan or Mr. Johnson. Mr. Snow'd never throw rocks at puppies. Why do you suppose he did it, Paul? A gentle man like Mr. Snow... Why'd he throw that brick through Mr. Sing's window?"

"'Cause he's scared, I guess."

"Scared of what? Of Mr. Sing? Nobody's scared of Mr. Sing."

"Naw, scared of the war. Scared Joe Bob's gonna get hurt. Killed maybe." He turned to look at me. "What we gotta do now is forget that we ever saw that brick. It sure wouldn't do anybody any good for us to go spillin' the beans. Three can keep a secret if tellin' it would hurt one of 'em real bad."

"You're right. I know you're right. But I wish we knew for sure that Mr. Snow wouldn't worry about us tellin'. He's got enough to worry about without that."

We both got quiet again.

It was up to me to start the forgetting. "Well, I don't know about you but I'm about to starve to death, and if we don't get to my house in a hurry, Mama's gonna say it's too close to supper time for cookies." I sniffed the air. "It's peanut butter today! I'm absolutely sure that today she made peanut butter! Last one there's John Alan's rotten lunch basket!"

CHAPTER 12
The Return of Paul's Father

When Paul and I charged in the back door of my house, we found my mother standing in front of an open oven, a sheet of peanut butter cookies in one hand and a spatula in the other. Things looked so ordinary, I decided it was going to be easy to forget Mr. Snow and the brick.

"See!" I slapped Paul on the arm. "While we were still inside the building, inside 5B, I told you there would be peanut butter cookies in this kitchen! Madam Zorina sees all, knows all!" Then I thought of Mr. Snow.

Mama slid the hot cookie sheet onto the stove

burners, switched off the radio, and forced a smile. The war news made her smiles harder to come by these days. I smiled back at her and tried to push thoughts of Mr. Snow away. Then I saw a half-written letter to Uncle Otis on the kitchen table next to a box she was about to fill with cookies to send to him. She took turns, a box to Uncle Otis one week, a box to Uncle Claude the next. The war filled even our kitchen table. Mr. Snow flittered over my brain again.

"Rachel, I know your daddy says you have a nose like a bloodhound, but I don't believe you knew they were peanut butter from six blocks away. She's making that up, isn't she, Paul?"

She waved the cookie on the spatula back and forth under my nose, dropped a napkin on my hand, and dumped the warm cookie in my palm. I held it up for inspection. "It ees zee design on zee top of zee peanut butter cookie which gives eet away," I said, trying to effect the accent of a French chef. "Gingerbread and sugar cookies 'ave no artificial markings. Zee tine of zee fork leaves a distinct odor!"

"Makes sense to me," Paul chimed in, opening his mouth just like the baby mockingbird he and I fed every day last summer when Sally Cat killed its mother. I pulled the soft warm wafer in two, stuffed the first half into my mouth, and dropped the other into Paul's. He chirped. "And she is telling the truth . . . for once. She did say they were peanut butter."

"My nose is a gift from Mother Nature," I muttered, swallowing my words along with my cookie. "It's her way of making up for the red hair."

"There's milk in the icebox and Ovaltine in the cupboard," Mama said as she scooped the rest of the cookies from the sheet and onto the rack before they could overcook. My mother is a very smart woman and a great cook, but she doesn't have a very modern vocabulary.

"It's called a *refrigerator* these days, Mother o' mine," I corrected her. "They stopped calling them iceboxes when Mr. Derby stopped delivering blocks of ice at the end of the Ice Age . . . way back when you were a child, remember?" *I bet Mr. Snow calls them iceboxes, too,* I thought.

"Don't irritate the cook," Paul told me as he untied Mama's apron strings, tugged her hair net off, and plopped down in a kitchen chair.

"Well, I'm happy to say that you two arrived just in time," she laughed, pulling the untied apron over her head and hanging it on the yellow butterfly hook on the wall. She plucked the hair net out of Paul's hand and stuck it in the apron pocket as she added,

"You incredibly smart kids can clean up this messy kitchen while I run to the store for the tomato sauce I forgot. We're having spaghetti for supper. And homemade French bread. And a salad. Want to stay, Paul?" she asked, as she did most nights.

"If you have apple pie for dessert, you'd better call John Alan and ask him over," Paul replied, getting up to pour us some milk. "That's the exact meal he never got to eat the day he lost his lunch basket." He was grinning at me so hard he almost ran the milk over the rim of the glass. Then he had to pour some milk back into the bottle to make room for the Ovaltine.

"Did Miss Cathcart ever find out who was tormenting poor little John Alan?" Mama wanted to know. "I've always had my own suspicions," she added, dropping another cookie in front of each of us and raising her eyebrows. Mr. Snow popped in my brain again. It would be a lot more fun to think about John Alan and his lunch basket than it was to think about Mr. Snow and that brick, so I closed my eyes and remembered.

It was the third Monday in September. School was back in session after our break for cotton picking. The room had been closed up airtight for two whole weeks. Mr. Snow was sick that day, so Miss Cathcart had to unlock the door to let us in. We were pushing and shoving each other, trying to be the first one in the room, but then we all stopped dead in our tracks.

"Pew-wee!" Billy Joe cried. "That's the worst smell I've ever smelled in all my born days! That's worse'n my little brother's toots after he's had beans and cabbage for breakfast, dinner, and supper all on the same day! He likes to sneak way down under the sheet and fart!"

"Billy Joe," Miss Cathcart admonished him as she rushed to open the windows. "Mind your mouth!"

"It's not my mouth I'm worried about," Billy Joe told her. "It's my nose." And he pinched it shut and used his Big Chief tablet for a fan.

"Why, it stinks worse'n that Easter egg that got hid in our old phonograph, the red one that didn't get found 'til May!" Jean Margaret chimed in. "Had a whole nickel stuck to it, but that egg smelled so rotten Mama throwed it away, nickel and all. Ever Easter Daddy tells how Mama throwed good money away just 'cause it stinked!"

"I do believe it's the long lost lunch basket," Kenneth said matter-of-factly. "Don't think I want to trade anything with you today, John Alan."

John Alan didn't think Kenneth's remark was

funny, but the rest of us did. He stood there narrowing his eyes at me, but I just clamped my nose and grinned.

We all knew the smell came from the missing lunch basket, but locating it was another matter entirely. The odor was so strong it had seeped into every nook and cranny of the room. We looked like those bloodhounds Sherlock Holmes uses as we made our way around the room, taking turns holding our noses and letting go to sniff or breathe. Paul, Kenneth, and I stayed as far away from the dictionary box as we could without arousing suspicion.

Miss Cathcart was the one who finally zeroed in on it. She lifted one corner of the dictionary box with her fingertips and immediately slapped it back shut. "John Alan," she said frantically, waving both hands in front of her face, "take this horrible smelly box out to the trash barrel immediately!"

He was really mad about that, but after all, it was his lunch basket. We all watched out the window as he pulled the dictionaries out one at a time holding his nose with one hand and the books with the other. He piled them on the ground next to the barrel. The lunch basket, however, was beyond saving. He stomped on it a bunch of times, crammed it down into the trash barrel, and stalked back to the room.

My revenge had been sweet, even though the smell was not, that hot day last September. I took a deep breath and was glad it was peanut butter cookies I was smelling now. Remembering that day had almost made me forget Mr. Snow and the brick entirely.

Just then, the telephone rang. I looked at Paul and he looked at me. We were both thinking the same thing. We hoped it wasn't Mr. Snow.

"Saved by the bell!" Paul hollered, slapping his hand on the kitchen table hard enough to make the cookies pop up in the air. "End of round five! Buddy Baer has just opened a gash over Defending Heavyweight Champ Joe Louis' left eye!" he continued in imitation of the sports broadcaster who reported the boxing matches. Paul shadowboxed the air in front of him, ducking and weaving in and out of the table and chairs while Mama went to the living room to answer the phone. He didn't look at me.

Mama came back very quickly. "Paul, it was your father. He's at your house. He said for you to come home right away."

Paul's arms dropped to his sides, and his eyes widened in amazement.

Paul's father often disappears for weeks at a time, and this time he had not been heard from since the day after Halloween, but we were not as amazed by his return as we were by his telephone call. He had never, in all the years we had known him, called our house on the telephone.

Mother looked from one to the other of us and tried to act as if it was a normal occurrence. "You can take this cookie with you," she added, wrapping one in a napkin as she spoke. "In fact, here's some more for your family," and she began filling my lunchbox, which I had just emptied, with the soft warm cookies. She knew they would all stick together with no paper between the layers, but I could tell she was too distracted to care.

"Rachel can take her lunch in a sack," she said absently as she handed my Roy Rogers lunchbox to Paul. Mama thinks food makes bad times better.

I tried to think of something cheerful to say, but no words would come.

"My father is home," Paul said slowly, as if he needed to hear his own voice repeat the news in order to believe that it was true. "And he called on the telephone..." He didn't bother to pull on his jacket. He just threw it over his arm, grabbed my cookie-filled lunchbox by the rope handle, picked up his books, and headed out the back door.

"Paul, it's awfully cold out there," Mama called out after him, but it was too late.

Paul was already gone. And neither of us was thinking about Mr. Snow anymore.

CHAPTER 13
Deported to California

I waited all weekend for Paul to call or come over to tell me what had happened, but I didn't hear a word from him. Mama wouldn't allow me to call him or go over to this house. "It's private family business," she said every time I begged, so it wasn't until Monday that I found out the awful truth.

It wasn't John Alan who was going to be deported.

It was Paul.

"California?" I wailed when I heard the news. "You can't move to California. You just can't!" We had just met at the corner halfway between our two houses, the same corner where we met every school day of every year since first grade except when we had the mumps when we were eight. "That may be the next place to get bombed! I won't let you move to California! I won't!"

"I haven't got any choice, Rachel," Paul said, staring off at the bank of smoky gray clouds that were rapidly rolling toward Apache from the north. "My father's made up his mind. We're moving to California. You know when my father makes up his mind about something, there's no changing it. 'Gee! Haw!' Remember?"

I remembered. Paul's Grandpa Griggs told us over and over, "Pauly, your pa is jist like that ol' mule, Albert, 'at I had when we lived back in Kansas. Wonst yore Pa makes up his mind, you can 'Gee!' in one ear and 'Haw!' in 'tother and it won't change nothin'." Just thinking about him made us both smile even now. He died last April, and we still missed him something awful. He was Paul's father's dad, but they were as different as day and night. Grandpa Griggs was steady and reliable. He was also real smart, even though he'd never finished high school. He read all the time and was always reading out loud to us. He made us memorize poems and sayings from *The Farmer's Almanac,* which he kept right next to his Bible.

When Paul's father disappeared, Grandpa Griggs would help Paul and his mom get by since she doesn't make much ushering and selling tickets at the picture show. But Grandpa Griggs had died, and there was nobody to help Paul and his mother now.

"Even Grandpa couldn't have changed Pop's mind about moving. He says there's gold just laying in the streets waiting for folks to scoop it up with a U.S. Government shovel," Paul said with a big sigh. "Even before Pearl Harbor, jobs in defense plants were payin' good money, and Pop talked about working in one. Now that there's a war on, he thinks he'll be a millionaire by summer. Heard some guy in a bar say that El Centro, California, was the place to go. 'There's a chicken in every pot in El Centro!' is how he put it. I told him I like my chicken fried not stewed," Paul added, trying to make a joke when there was nothing left in the world that was funny.

"But why do you and your mom have to go with him?" I said, the lump in my throat growing bigger by the minute. "He's gone off by himself a hundred times before."

"He says Mom can get a really good job, too, and he needs her to cook and clean while he works double shifts. She's supposed to work double shifts, too, and then cook and clean. It's crazy. You know Pop and

132

work. Granddad always said Pop wanted a job with all the work picked out. But he's already got cardboard boxes stacked all over our house. He was slinging stuff into them when I left and singing 'California, Here I Come!' so loud the neighbors could hear."

Just then Paul spied a pine cone in the middle of the sidewalk. He went over and kicked it so hard that it almost hit a dog that was loping down the other side of the street. "We'd be leaving next week if he hadn't had to give our landlord notice and get the utilities turned off." He got that funny faraway look on his face that he seems to have more and more often as he added, "I'm pretty sure that this is really my fault . . . something I did . . ." His voice trailed off.

"Now, how could it be your fault?" I said, trying to figure out what he was talking about. "You haven't done anything wrong."

He kept looking down at the ground.

"Hey! Maybe they'd let you stay here and live with us. My folks wouldn't mind. I know they wouldn't. We can go ask them right now," I said, pulling the sleeve of his jacket. "We can be late to school today."

"Oh, Rachel, it's no use. Mom's so upset over this, I couldn't ask her to let me stay here. She needs me. Needs me bad. He's goin' with her to Mr. Burns' house this morning to make sure she quits. Then she'll have to go. I have to go. It's what I deserve."

I didn't understand what he meant about the deserving part, but I did understand about his mother. None of that helped the way I was feeling. How was I going to survive the war without Paul to talk to?

We trudged on down the street, the wind pushing at our backs and the clouds taking turns blotting out the sun. Even Mr. Snow and his "yah" brick were forgotten.

The bell had already rung by the time we reached the schoolyard. John Alan was nowhere to be seen, and for the first time in a long while, I didn't even care or wonder where he was. Once Paul was gone, I wouldn't have my second witness anyway—so what did it matter?

Mr. Snow would probably be glad to hear that Paul was having to move. One less person around who knew his secret. "Three may keep a secret if two of them are dead." We had put that on the blackboard. Paul wasn't dead, but it seemed to me that his being in California was almost as bad.

CHAPTER 14
The Two Sams

As I trudged to meet Paul on the corner the next morning, I could barely keep my eyes open. All night long I had the worst dreams I've ever had. Mr. Snow was chasing me down the street, and he had a brick in each hand. He was yelling "Yah! Yah! Yah!" at the top of his lungs. Then Mr. Johnson jumped out from behind a bush and started trying to hit me over the head with an American flag. I ran and ran as fast as I could, but there were bombs dropping all around me, and John Alan appeared and was about to shove my face down into his rotten-smelling lunch basket when Sally Cat jumped in the middle of my stomach and woke me up. For once I was really glad Al had stuck her in my room so she'd wake *me* up instead of him. I yawned and trudged on down the street.

Paul was waiting for me under the Flying Red Horse sign on Mr. Johnson's station. I had seen that sign a million times before, but I had never taken the time to read the part in small letters right under the horse's left hoof. It was a little sign hanging from two chains and it read "B. Arnold Johnson, Proprietor."

"Paul, look at that!" I squealed, pointing up to the sign, really happy to have something to talk about instead of Mr. Snow or Paul moving to California. "Look at Mr. Johnson's name! I have been trying to find out what it is, and there it is, right there on that sign! B. Arnold Johnson. He's a traitor just like John Alan Feester! With a name like Benedict Arnold Johnson, he's bound to be guilty of something big!"

"Lucky for you I just saw Mr. B. Arnold Johnson go in the outhouse," Paul said in a loud whisper as he grabbed my arm and led me down the sidewalk at a fast clip. "Otherwise he'd be chunkin' a rock at you right this minute for talkin' about him so loud and clear. Some spy you are. Come on. Let's get as far away from here as fast as we can without arousing suspicion."

We waited until we got to the end of the block before we said anything more. I could hardly stand it.

"Paul! His name!"

"Rachel, we don't know that the B stands for Benedict. It could be Benjamin or Barney or even Bobby."

"Nobody's name is really Bobby, Paul. If his name was Bobby it would really be Robert and the sign would say 'R. Arnold Johnson.' Robert Arnold Johnson would not be guilty of anything, but Benedict Arnold Johnson is. Anyway, while we are standing here arguing about his name, he's probably dropping vital evidence down the hole in the outhouse, and we'll never find it!" I told him with a stamp of my foot. "Before you move we've gotta search every inch of that filling station, front to back, top to bottom for evidence. We know Mr. Johnson is a prime suspect because he is not the least bit patriotic. He never puts up a flag. And how about all that exercising? An old man like him—why he's at least forty—why would he be exercising all the time if he didn't think he was going to have to run away from something? This may be the very last Secret Squadron mission we ever get to have together in our whole entire lives. You know I'm gonna do it by myself if you don't help me! I guess you don't care if I get caught!"

"Aw, Rachel, don't put it that way. When you say

it that way, you know that I'll give in." He stopped and looked down at the ground for a minute, gave a big sigh, and then he looked back up at me. "Okay, okay, we'll break into Benedict Arnold Johnson's Flying Red Horse filling station and probably get caught and thrown in jail for the rest of our lives. At least I won't have to move to California and maybe they'll give us adjoining cells in Big Mac. That's what they call the penitentiary in McAlester, Big Mac. You need to know facts like that if that's where your mail's gonna be goin' before long."

"Oh, Paul. They'd never send a couple of kids like us to the penitentiary even if we got caught, which we won't. Before I even saw that sign I had decided that Mr. Johnson was probably in cahoots with John Alan, that he was a spy like that Major André, the one who got hung. Only Mr. Johnson is the Benedict Arnold and John Alan may just have to get hung!"

"But Rachel, if your theory about John Alan and the sneak attacks is right, that means John Alan tipped over the outhouse with his own fellow spy, traitor, or saboteur in it. How do you explain that and the fact that neither one of them has an accent?"

"Oh, they just did that to throw us off the track! So we'd think they didn't like each other. That's the oldest trick in the book, Paul. And I haven't figured it out about the accent. Maybe they got people to give 'em speech training so they sound like Americans! Captain Midnight talked about stuff like that just last week. Saboteurs can be taught to talk like Americans, but they don't know how to think like us. Now, meet me at noon under the flagpole, and we'll start plotting it out. And if you see Mr. Snow, just act normal, remember? Just act normal."

"I'm not the one who has trouble acting normal, Rachel. Look in the mirror!"

We met at both recesses and at noon but by the time school was out and we were headed home to listen to Captain Midnight, Paul was getting cold feet again. At least neither one of us had run into Mr. Snow. Somebody said they thought he was sick, and that had us a little worried.

"What if we get caught, Rachel? We're already kind of harboring a criminal, not tellin' about Mr. Snow and the brick. What are you gonna say to your father when they call him down to the jail to say that his daughter was caught crawling out the window of the Flying Red Horse filling station in the middle of the night with a flashlight in her mouth?"

"We will not get caught. And if we are, I'll be able to convince them that we're right about Benedict

Arnold Johnson being a traitor to his country. Then the police will help us look for evidence! But if we find his diary in there, and Mr. Johnson confesses in it that he's dropped vital evidence down the outhouse hole, it's gonna be *you* they lower to the bottom on a rope to look for it, not me!"

"I knew it! I knew it! The only reason you want me in on this is so I'm the one who has to go down on the rope!" He held his nose and began to laugh and it seemed like old times—old times before the war, before we were having to worry about California or Mr. Snow. Then he got serious again.

"You know what we haven't done yet, don't ya? We haven't gone by Mr. Sing's to tell him we were sorry about the window like Miss Cathcart told everybody to do. I haven't gone because I didn't want to have to look at him, knowing what I know. You haven't mentioned it, so I'm guessin' you haven't gone either, right? But if we're the only two people in the class who don't do what she told us to do, she's gonna wonder why. She said we were to report back to her. Don't think our helping him clean up counts."

"I know we gotta, but that's gonna be harder than sneakin' in the Flying Red Horse. Besides the fact that we know who threw the brick, we were as bad as Mr. Snow, thinkin' that John Alan might have been takin' secret plans to Mr. Sing's laundry. Maybe we shoulda told Mr. Snow that, you know." I looked down at the ground and then back up at Paul. "We'll go by Mr. Sing's right after Captain Midnight. I don't think the laundry closes 'til 5:30." We walked in the house just in time to flip on the radio.

As the program opened, Captain Midnight and Chuck Ramsey were talking about an experimental infrared viewing device they had that would allow members of the Secret Squadron to observe things in the dark. It was made for them to use outdoors on moonless nights, but Paul and I started talking about how great it would be if we had one like it to take with us into the Flying Red Horse filling station. Joyce Ryan had some night glasses that would be a big help, too. Joyce always has just as much of the good equipment as the guys do. They always treat her fair and equal. That was one big reason I liked the program so much.

"Wish there were some way we could borrow stuff like that from them, don't you?" I asked Paul. "I know Joyce would loan me her stuff if she could. She's the best shot they've got, even without those glasses."

Paul grinned at me and shook his head.

"I know! I know! They are not real people, but

most of what they say is real. And if they could know about Pearl Harbor before it even happened, they probably really do have something that lets them see in the dark, so there!" I looked at my watch. "Well, we've put it off as long as we can. Let's go to the laundry and get it over with."

Neither of us was in any great hurry, so we started playing "That's mine!" in all the store windows we passed. That's a stupid game we played when we were little kids, but we still like to do it when there's nobody else around to hear and make fun. It's really pretty dumb because all you do is point to things and say "That's mine!" and the first person who does it gets whatever it is. Of course, nobody really *gets* anything because it's just a silly game, and we don't have any money, but we play it anyway. I had already gotten two clock radios, a Monopoly game, and a set of binoculars, and Paul had gotten one radio and a penknife. We didn't wish for the same things as much anymore, so it wasn't as much fun as when we were little kids and had fights over who said "That's mine" first.

Before we really wanted to be there, we were standing in front of Sam Sing's boarded-up window. The words "I'm Chinese!" stared down at us. The boards kept us from being able to see into the shop.

The little Oriental bells on the door jingled as we shoved it open. There was Mr. Snow standing in front of Sam Sing. Mr. Snow had both of his hands out in front of him. One held a fist full of money. In the palm of the other lay the "yah" brick.

They both turned to see who had come in. Nobody said a word.

Mr. Snow handed the brick to Mr. Sing, who took it with both hands even though it was not very big or heavy. Sam Sing held that brick as if it were a wonderful present. Mr. Snow just stood there and looked from Sam to Paul to me. Then he put five one-dollar bills on the counter, smoothing each one down as carefully as if he were Sam ironing a white silk shirt.

Finally, Mr. Snow spoke. "The girl here says you come to Oklahoma 'cause you wanted ta be a cowboy."

Mr. Sing nodded his head enthusiastically. "Cowboy! Yes! Sam Sing, blare black lider! Yero blare black lider!" He smiled broadly. "Horses not aglee with Sam Sing!" He laughed out loud this time.

"Horses not aglee with Sam Snow either," Mr. Snow replied.

"Sam?" Mr. Sing shouted out. "You Sam, too? Me Sam! You Sam! Two of klind!"

"Two of klind!" Mr. Snow agreed.

Everything got very quiet again.

"Well," Mr. Snow said finally. "Guess I better git on home to supper. Mrs. Snow'll be waitin' on me."

"Come clean!" Sam Sing sang out as he always did when a customer left. It was his little "American joke," he told my father. Funny... It seemed like that was what poor old Mr. Snow had just done, "Come clean." But why had he done it? Why had he brought the brick to Mr. Sing?

"It was 'cause of these kids I come," Mr. Snow said, as if he had read my mind. "They saw the brick in my closet and promised not ta tell. Didn't say as much out loud, but I knew that's what they was bittin' around the edges about. Made me want to make it right by you. I'll bring ya five dollars ever month 'til the glass is paid up." He stepped back, pulled his old gray stocking cap out of his pocket, and pulled it on. "I'll let the three of you figure out what to do with that brick." He turned and started out the door, but then he turned back. "Three can keep a secret, can't they? Even if they're all alive and kickin'." And he was gone.

Sam looked from Paul to me and back again.

"Just us, okay? Just me and you and you," he said, pointing to each of us in turn.

"Sure," Paul told him, as I shook my head up and down.

"Cross my heart and hope to die, stick red peppers in my eye," I added, crossing my heart as I went along. I knew there was no way I could explain the red pepper part, but I could tell by the way Mr. Sing crossed his own heart that he knew what that silly little American rhyme meant.

He reached under the counter and got out a beautiful little black box. It had golden birds painted on the lid and a tiny gold clasp. He undid the clasp and opened it as if he were performing a magic trick. Inside was the broken brick with "Sequo" on it. He picked it up, put it on the counter, and carefully fitted the "yah" brick in its place. He stared at it as if he were willing the two pieces back together.

Then he picked up a piece in each hand and handed them to Paul.

"Get lid of 'ese fol the Sams, okay?"

"Okay," Paul told him as he shoved a piece into each pocket of his jacket. "Let's go, Rachel."

"Come clean!" Mr. Sing shouted as we walked out the door.

CHAPTER 15
Bricks Away!

"Well, Captain Midnight, I wonder where you can dispose of that broken brick so that nobody in the whole wide world would ever find it?" I giggled as Paul and I walked down the street toward my house. It wasn't quite dark yet, but it would be soon. "Perhaps you could drop it from the plane."

"No, Joyce," he replied in a great imitation of Captain Midnight's voice, "I have a better idea. The Squadron is planning a 'visit' to the Flying Red Horse filling station. I think it would be a good idea for me to check out the surrounding area first... places like the *outhouse,* where possible un-American activities might be taking place."

"Pardon me, Captain," I replied, trying to sound as much like the no-nonsense Joyce as I could, "but up until now, outhouses have never been discussed on this program. In fact, the Apache Secret Squadron, located in the state of Oklahoma, may be the only squadron in the world with any secret information on outhouses. Would you like for me to request their help? Or, sir, I'd be happy to assist you myself. I have these new glasses which allow me to see in the dark. Few outhouses, I've been told, have electricity."

"No, Joyce, it is my understanding that this is a one-holer, therefore it's a one-man job. It might look a bit suspicious if the two of us entered the outhouse together, each with a brick in hand, don't you think? Especially with you in those see-in-the-dark glasses."

By this time we were both laughing so hard we were wobbling down the street like the Tyson brothers when they've had too much to drink.

"How come you get all the fun?" I teased, holding my nose and remembering how much I hated to use the outhouse at my grandparents' house. "The honor is all yours, but I do hope you will have some Words of Wisdom ready to intone when you drop them!"

"Oh, I already thought of that. I'll just hold one in each hand in the air for an appropriate length of time... one second should be enough since with both hands occupied I can't hold my nose... and shout 'Bricks Away!' as they drop through the hole. 'Bricks Away!' Like 'Bombs Away!' Get it?"

I got it.

He slapped me on the back and headed for the outhouse in back of the Flying Red Horse.

I was gonna miss him so bad.

CHAPTER 16
A Long Way to California

Now that the mystery over the brick thrower had been solved, we were back to trying to get into the Christmas spirit with the world at war and Paul packing up to move to California. We were still planning to sneak into the Flying Red Horse, but even that idea didn't seem as exciting as it had before school was out. If I was going to be able to connect John Alan Feester, traitor, to B. Arnold Johnson, spy, I didn't have much time left to do it with Paul's help. Just thinking about it was beginning to make me tired.

I woke up on the Monday after school let out for vacation feeling the color of a bottle of Mrs. Stewart's Bluing. I never have figured out how that dark blue liquid makes clothes whiter, but Mama pours some in every load she washes. She says it brightens her clothes. I wondered if pouring some of it on me would brighten my spirits. Probably it would just turn my skin as blue as I felt.

I put off getting up for as long as I could, but finally the smell of bacon frying and hash-browned potatoes in the skillet pulled my nose downstairs to the kitchen and the rest of me had to follow.

"Isn't your daddy lookin' for you down at *The Republican*?" Mama asked, glancing at her watch as she poured my milk. She buttered my toast, and I watched as she cut the bread in the same eternally boring rectangular pieces. I don't know why she can't cut my toast in triangles like they do in restaurants. I've told her a million times, but she claims it's hard to break old habits. Paul says bread cut from one corner to the other tastes better to him, also, but his mom always cuts it wrong, too. Who was I going to complain to about toast when he was gone?

"Paul and I are both goin'," I told her, dumping in the Ovaltine and stirring it around and around. "Daddy said he needed us both today." I put the spoon on my plate and watched the sweet brown liquid slide right into the poached egg and the toast. Soggy toast, sugary egg. I didn't care.

"That's good," Mama said, spooning hash browns on to my plate next to the crisp bacon strips. Mama is a really good cook, and she believes in a good breakfast as much as she believes in castor oil.

"Daddy and I know that you and Paul need to make the most of the time you've got left before he moves. I know how sad this is for you, Rachel. Good friends like Paul are real hard to come by. Daddy and I'll miss him, too, you know. Wish we could do something to help." She patted me on the head, sat down across from me, and took a long sip from her Will Rogers coffee mug. I won it at the State Fair tossing pennies. The worry lines in her forehead seemed to get deeper by the day.

I picked up last Wednesday's edition of *The Republican*, which was on top of the wastebasket, and read "Peace on Earth" in bold black type across the top of Woodward's Hardware store ad. It didn't seem to me that there was peace anywhere on earth, not even in my own family. After two whole weeks of arguing, Daddy finally convinced Al that he had to finish high school before he went into the army. That caused a temporary truce and took one of my worries away for the time being. Surely this war would be over by the time Al graduated. That would be a whole year and a half away.

Uncle Claude and Uncle Otis were both on alert status, which Mama says means that they have to be ready to ship out anywhere, anytime. They keep moving them around so much she has trouble figuring out where to send the cookies. There sure wasn't much peace on my grandma's earth—she had no idea where her sons would be by the end of December.

Even my usually cheerful, talkative Mama was quiet these days. She got up, filled the sink with hot soapy water, and started to wash the dishes.

"You don't need to dry today," she told me. "I'll let 'em air dry in the rack. Go meet Paul, and you all help your daddy. It'll keep your mind off other things." She kept washing the same red plate over and over.

I finished my breakfast and plodded back upstairs to my room. I brushed my teeth with Pepsodent and tried to flash a smile to the redhead who stared back at me, but I couldn't make the corners of my mouth go up. I pulled at my lips with my fingers, but that didn't work either. I made my bed, pulled on my green plaid shirt and some warm slacks, and headed back down the stairs. I heard our old grandfather clock strike nine times and realized I was late. Daddy had asked us to be at the shop by 9:00. I grabbed my coat and pulled it on as I ran out the front door. I took the steps two at a time and sprinted all the way to the corner. Paul was waiting for me. He was scuffing the toes of his shoes on the sidewalk and staring at the ground.

"Hey! Why so glum, chum?" I said, trying to catch my breath.

"Last night we got the final word," he said, blowing his breath out in a big sigh which frosted in the cold December air. The temperature had dropped during the night and the wind had picked up. "Moving day is January 1," he groaned. "That's the day I get deported!"

"Tell me his exact words."

Hooking his fingers in imaginary suspenders and rocking back and forth on his heels, Paul launched into an imitation of his father. "On New Year's Day, January 1, 1942, before the sun hits the back windshield of that old Chevy, we'll hit the end of that driveway, and we'll race all those other Okies all the way to Californy! Within six months we'll be able to buy the whole danged state!" He looked and sounded so much like his father that I started laughing in spite of myself. Paul's great at imitations.

"Well, now we know for sure. That means we have almost two whole weeks of vacation before you have to go," I said trying to sound cheerful as we started to walk toward town. "We can walk in on John Alan Feester's top-secret meeting with B. Arnold Johnson, discover the original plans for the bombing of Pearl Harbor in the Flying Red Horse, and listen to 'Captain Midnight' together every day it's on."

"It's only nine days, not two weeks. And we listen to 'Captain Midnight' together almost every day, anyway," Paul pointed out. "What's so different about listening together during Christmas vacation?"

"Well, I thought we could pretend that you were already in California and I was here and every day at the very same time you would be listening and I would be listening so I could picture exactly what you were doing. That way, at least once a day, we wouldn't have to be wondering what the other person was doing because we would know. The other person would be listening to 'Captain Midnight.'"

"But California is not in the same time zone as Oklahoma," Paul pointed out. "When it's four o'clock in California, it's six o'clock in Oklahoma. There's a pretty good chance the radio stations out there broadcast the program at an earlier time, so I might hear 'Captain Midnight' an hour or two before you do." And for the first time since he found out that he was moving, Paul Griggs laughed loud and long.

154

"You mean you might know what happens before I do every single day?" I wailed.

"I'm afraid so," Paul said, trying to sound real sorry but not doing a very good job of it. "How about if I write you a letter the minute the program is over and tell you exactly how Joyce's see-in-the-dark glasses allowed her to keep Ivan Shark from killing Captain Midnight that day?"

"A lot of good that will do me since it takes about a hundred years for a letter to get from California to Oklahoma." There was a long pause while we both contemplated the incredible distance which would soon separate us. "How long do you think it takes... for a letter, I mean?"

"Four or five days at least, maybe a week even if we don't send them airmail. Airmail is pretty expensive." Paul sighed a big sigh and his eyes got a real faraway look—a look like he was already in California and was trying to see all the way back here.

"I bet my parents'll let me call you long distance on your birthday," I told him trying to think of something good to say. "I've never made a long distance call in my life. I don't even know how, but I bet I can learn. And February is not that far away. Nineteen forty-two is the year our birthdays are both on

Friday the thirteenth, remember? Our lucky days. That oughta make 'em special enough that they'll let us call long distance."

"I don't think they're gonna be lucky days, Rachel. Don't think any of my days in California will be lucky ones. Besides that, long-distance calls cost a whole lot of money," Paul said, chewing his lip. "Nobody I know makes long-distance calls unless somebody's died or is in really bad trouble. Besides, my father said we probably won't even have a telephone in California. Won't know anybody to call out there. Daddy says Mama's gonna be so busy working and counting her money that she won't have time to gossip on the phone like she does here. He hates her talkin' on the phone. She cries all the time. Says she's leaving everything she loves but me."

"You're not even going to have a *telephone*?" I moaned. "So even if I had a *bad* emergency, even if John Alan had me locked up in a closet and set the house on fire, I couldn't call you to come rescue me?"

"Rachel, if you were locked in a burning closet, you couldn't call me even if I still lived in Apache," Paul said, laughing out loud again. "You've got Captain Midnight on the brain."

"But what if I find the proof that we need to

expose John Alan as a dirty rotten traitor? How will I ever be able to bring him to justice by myself? "

We had just reached the front door of *The Republican.*

"You can get your father to put it in the paper," Paul told me. "I can see the headline now: 'Rachel the Resister Foils John Alan Feester!'"

"Much too long for a headline," I pointed out, counting the imaginary letters in the air. "Have to cut it way down. Wait! Wait! I got it! You know how well I speak French. Well, we'll do the headline in French! How about 'Reester Foils Feester!' It even rhymes!"

We opened the door laughing and trying to pretend that our world was not falling apart.

CHAPTER 17
Greetings from the President!

"Well, it's about time!" Daddy boomed. "We're on deadline here, you two! Big news! Roosevelt's signing an amended Selective Service Act today. Extending the draft to all men from twenty to *forty-four*. Even more amazing, every man between eighteen and *sixty-four* has to register, even the president of the United States himself!"

Paul and I turned to look at each other, our mouths dropping open at the same time. "Every man between eighteen and sixty-four? Even Mr. Franklin D. Roosevelt?" Paul repeated. "That means my father! That means even you, Mr. Dalton. Between eighteen and sixty-four years old!"

"I'd be proud to defend our country, Paul," Daddy told him, "but having to register doesn't mean you're up for the draft. Just means thcy want to know where every man in that age bracket is living and how many of us there are. Don't think they'll take an old man like me. At least not yet."

"My father says he won't ever have to go," Paul said, looking down at the floor. "Says his bad back'll keep him out. And him only thirty-one. Don't see how they'd find him anyway. Won't have an address before long."

"Well, gotta have a strong back to go to war," Daddy said, trying to make Paul feel better. He began pacing back and forth in front of the old pot-bellied stove. "Prime Minister Winston Churchill and his staff have just arrived in the U.S. from England. Roosevelt's called a joint press conference for tomorrow. It's getting hard to keep up, there's so much goin' on at once. I got an editorial galloping around in my head I need to get down on paper before it wears itself out." He paused to take a deep breath and shake his hands. He's starting to get arthritis in his fingers, and cold weather makes them stiff. Makes it hard for him to type.

"Paul, can you clean up my typewriter for me? I dropped a box of paperclips right into the key well, and some of 'em are stuck between the keys. Real mess! May have a hard time fishing 'em all out. I know Rachel doesn't have the patience." He turned to me. "And Rachel, while he's doin' that, I need you to do some research. Last year, Congress passed the first peacetime selective service program. Caused a real big stink. I 'member the date was October 16 'cause it was a Wednesday, paper day for *The Republican*. Had a dickens of a time thinking up a banner headline to remind every man twenty-one to thirty-six of his patriotic duty. Too many letters! Can't remember what I came up with. Now I need you to find the exact date in September that the Burke-Wadsworth Act, that was the name of it, was passed. I need that date for my editorial. If I don't have my facts straight, some smart reader will be happy to point out my mistake, believe you me."

I believed him. Nothing upset Daddy more than to have an error in his paper, and it didn't happen very often. He was a stickler for detail. We keep all the old copies of *The Republican* filed in metal frames in the little storage room on the northeast corner of the office. They are in flat bins that slide out and are filed by the months and years. I pulled out September of 1940 and began to search. Since our paper is a weekly, it didn't take me long to find what he needed.

"September 16," I called out so he could hear me from the back room. "It was called the Selective Training and Service Act. You're right about that other date, too. On October 16 every man between the ages of twenty-one and thirty-six had to sign up."

It was like riding a time machine backward to look at those headlines about the war from a year ago and know what I knew now about Pearl Harbor. I ran my fingers up, down, and across the pages, reading headlines and opening paragraphs. I stopped on October 27, 1940.

"Listen to this, Paul, my history hungry friend, it's from October last year: 'On the twenty-ninth, President Franklin Roosevelt will appear in Washington, D.C., to witness the selection of the first draft numbers from the more than sixteen million men who registered on October 16.' Sixteen million men! Says here that's more than twice the population of New York City! The last sentence reads, 'The military plans to have more than a million troops ready for action in a year.' This paper is dated October 27, 1940, more than a year before the Japanese bombed Pearl Harbor! Why did they decide to do that a whole year ago, Daddy?"

161

"War's been coming at us for a long time, Punkin, and Roosevelt knew it. And he knew we weren't even close to being ready. It's a good thing for America that he pushed so hard for the draft. Believe me, he got lots of opposition in Congress as well as from the people. It's hard to admit it, but he's the man for the job, even if he is a Democrat."

I was amazed to hear Daddy say Roosevelt was right about anything, because Daddy is such a big Republican. He even taught our bulldog, Jeep, a Republican trick. He would say, "Jeep, would you rather be a dead dog or a Democrat?" and Jeep would fall down on the ground, roll over on his back and stick both feet straight up in the air. It was a great trick, especially in an election year like 1940, when the Democrats were winning everything.

"What's 'conscripted' mean, Daddy? The lead paragraph of this article says the men were conscripted."

"Conscripted's just another word for drafted, Punkin. Has eleven letters instead of seven, so it takes up more space in a headline. Four letters are a lot. That reminds me. We're going to have to rewrite all of the headlines. We'll make conscripted your word for today. Missed giving you one at breakfast since you slept late. Look it up in Webster's. Use it in the headline if you can."

Daddy gave me a grim smile as he wiped his hands on the apron he wore to keep the printer's ink off his clothes. Mama claims that printer's ink is the "bane of her existence." When I asked what that meant, Daddy made "bane" my word for the day, and I found out that it means "pain." I didn't understand that at all. I couldn't believe Mama thought anything about printer's ink was bad. It smells as good as "Midnight in Paris" cologne to me. Once when I was little, I saw Mama dab perfume behind her ears, so the next day at Daddy's office, I put printer's ink behind my ears. I found out about bane and pain when Mama tried to scrub it off. It was months before that stain wore off my fingers and my neck, and Daddy grinned every time he saw it.

I was just about to slide the drawer shut when the headline "Service Station Sold" caught my eye. I began to read: "The Flying Red Horse service station was sold this week to Beauregard Arnold Johnson of Sequoyah, who . . ." I stopped reading and looked over to where Paul was working on Daddy's typewriter. I stood there a full minute trying to decide whether or not I should call him back and show him. Then I slid the drawer closed.

"Has there been more news about the USS *Oklahoma*?" I asked Daddy. "It's been over two weeks now! Seems to me that somebody should know all the facts about it and Pearl Harbor by now!"

"Oh, I'm sure President Roosevelt and the military people know a lot of things they are not telling, Punkin. When you're in a war, lots of facts become 'military secrets.' The longer we can keep the enemy from knowing how much damage was done at Pearl, the better for everybody on our side. It'll come out eventually, but it's going to take time and a lot of it. About got my typewriter ready to roll, Paul?"

"I'm down to the last one, Mr. Dalton. Got this rascal at last," he said with a sigh of relief as he flipped a clip into the air with a tongue depressor he had gotten out of Daddy's first-aid kit. "Been working on this last one off and on since I started. It's like that third out in the ninth inning, the hardest one to come by. It's stuck way down in the slot between the 'u' and the 'n' so it clogs up everything. Only solution may be ta mix up a magic potion to pour down in there, some kinda disappearin' ink. Shirley Jean says John Alan Feester, Junior, has the formula."

Just as he said that, the front door of the newspaper office flew open, and John Alan Feester, Junior, himself blew in.

"Did I hear someone call my name?"

CHAPTER 18
The Swiss Army Knife

"Well, hello, there Mr. Feester, Junior," my daddy said in a jovial tone of voice which should have never been used to address a possible spy, traitor, or saboteur. But then Daddy didn't know John Alan like I did.

"My father was going to bring this school board report down to you," John Alan replied, placing an envelope in my father's hands, "but I told him I would be happy to do it for him. I told him I always enjoyed visiting the offices of Apache's finest newspaper." He smiled broadly and waited for my father's thanks, which was quick in coming.

I was immediately suspicious. John Alan was rarely if ever helpful to anybody unless he wanted something.

Why would he volunteer to come to our newspaper office early in the morning on a cold Monday morning during the holidays? He was spying, that was what he was doing! He eyed the three of us huddled around Daddy's typewriter, so he moseyed our way.

"Hello, Rachel. Hello, Paul," he said in that fakey, good-natured tone he uses when grownups are around. "I hope you two are enjoying your Christmas vacation," he went on in the same silky chocolate-syrup voice. "I guess this will be your last Christmas in Oklahoma, won't it, Paul?" he purred just like Sally does when she wants to be fed. "I am so sorry to hear you are moving."

My father looked at me and raised his eyebrows as if to say, "And this is the kid you say is so bad?" My father was just as easy to fool as George Washington had been.

"I think I hear the ten o'clock train pulling in the station, John Alan," I retorted. "Why don't you go down and put a penny on the track, and maybe your neck, too?" I watched a frown cross Daddy's face.

But John Alan just chuckled and directed his reply to my father. "Your daughter is as funny as Jack Benny," he said, smiling the Pepsodent smile. "She and I have a great time kidding each other, don't we, Rachel?"

"We are real busy, John Alan," I answered through clenched teeth. "I would love to chat with you, but Paul and I have got to get this typewriter fixed so Daddy can write his editorial for tomorrow. We are on deadline," I told him with great authority.

"What's wrong with it?" Public Enemy Feester wanted to know, and I knew immediately that I had talked too much. Why had I mentioned our typewriter troubles?

"Oh, I accidentally dropped a box of paperclips in the key well, and Paul's got 'em all out but one," Daddy informed him, without realizing that all of that information might be valuable to the enemy. Captain Midnight's Secret Squadron members would never have revealed all those important details to someone who was a prime suspect.

"I'll bet I've got something to *aid* you," said Possible Traitor #1, who had just today become the world's most helpful kid. He whipped out what looked like an enormous pocketknife. It seemed to appear out of nowhere. "This is a Swiss army knife," he informed us. "With it I can fix anything." He peered inside the typewriter as he began to unfold the various blades.

What was he talking about when he said he was going to *aid* us? What kind of remark was that? What if he had really been sent by the Swiss government to sabotage my father's newspaper with that Swiss army knife? Captain Midnight talked about saboteurs all the time. If John Alan wasn't a traitor or a spy, maybe he was a saboteur! If the local people didn't know what was going on in the world, it would be a whole lot easier to invade their town. Or their country! I just realized that one of the most important places to sabotage would be the local newspaper! Keep the town's people in the dark!

"Don't you touch my daddy's typewriter!" I hollered. "Don't you dare lay a finger on it, you saboteur, you! You and that Benedict Arnold Johnson spy friend of yours. Go back to the Flying Red Horse where you belong!"

"Rachel, what has gotten into you?" Daddy said, stepping close enough to put his hand on my shoulder and squeeze. "John Alan is just trying to be helpful, and I, for one, appreciate it."

I looked at Paul, who just shrugged his shoulders and rolled his eyes to the ceiling. I could never get him to back me up when it came to John Alan.

John Alan came to the section he was searching for in his fancy knife. He pulled it out, took the long-handled, tweezer-like instrument between his thumb and index finger, reached inside the typewriter, and easily extracted the last paperclip. He did it just as smoothly as Dr. O'Conner had pulled one of my baby teeth when the string-on-the-doorknob trick wouldn't work.

Without saying a word but trying very hard to keep a smirk off his face, John Alan swaggered across the room, handed the last pesky paperclip to my father, and strolled out the front door.

"Well," my father said, giving me a stern look, "what do you have to say for yourself, young lady? What in the world got into you? And what was that remark about John Alan being a saboteur and Mr. Johnson from the filling station being a spy? Have you taken leave of your senses?"

"Nothing. Not a thing," I said, my head hanging down. But my mind was spinning in a hundred different directions. Was John Alan a saboteur instead of a traitor or maybe both? Where had he gotten a Swiss army knife? Did you have to be in the Swiss army to own a knife like that? Which side was Switzerland on in the war anyway? The only thing I knew about Switzerland was where it was on a map. The minute Paul and I finished helping Daddy, we had to find out how John Alan had acquired a Swiss army knife.

"Well, I'll say this much, Rachel Elizabeth,"

Daddy said, pointing his finger at me, "I was embarrassed by your actions toward John Alan just now. I don't know what is going on between the two of you, but for the life of me I can't understand why you can't manage to get along with him. He seems like a very nice young man, a real gentleman. I'm beginning to suspect that *you* are the troublemaker."

A gentleman? John Alan Feester, a gentleman? I knew better than to try to change Daddy's mind. Not today, anyway. John Alan was always polite in front of adults.

"I'm sorry, Daddy. I never meant to embarrass you."

"Well, we've got work to do, so let's get with it," Daddy said, giving a big shrug. He sat down at his typewriter. "You know what needs doing, you've done it often enough." He started to peck away. He only uses two fingers, but he can type faster with those two than most people can using ten.

We all settled into our jobs, but that story I had seen in the files about the Flying Red Horse began picking the edges of my brain like a fingernail working on a scab. I knew it was going to draw blood eventually.

"Paul, come here a minute, would you?" I said, putting down the subscription list I was working on and leading him to the file closet. I pulled open the drawer for 1940. "Look what I found," I told him, pointing to the article. "You're right, again." He read the article.

"Beauregard Arnold Johnson, huh? Beauregard was a big hero for the South in the Civil War," he told me with a smirk. "He was the superintendent of the Military Academy at West Point, but that was long after Benedict Arnold left town. Beauregard. Don't blame him for callin' himself Arnold. Well, at least now we know what the B stands for." He went back to his headline writing.

With that scab taken care of, my mind started looking for another one. The thought that this was the last day Paul would be working with Daddy and me popped up like a cork, and I shoved it back down. Paul had been a part of our family and our newspaper for so long, I couldn't imagine either of them without him. I tried to pull in bad thoughts about John Alan and his fancy Swiss army knife, but even that didn't take my mind off of Paul's moving and how much I was going to miss him. Nothing did.

CHAPTER 19
"...aid and comfort..."

Paul and I didn't finish helping Daddy until a little after 3:00 P.M. Daddy got over being mad at me pretty quickly. He always does, but I knew he was still puzzled about me calling John Alan a saboteur and Mr. Johnson a spy. I coulda bit my tongue off for saying that out loud. Now that John Alan knew I suspected him, he'd be watching my every move. And Daddy would come straight to me if he heard about anything going on at the Flying Red Horse. The red-headed temper I claim I don't have pretty well ruined that plan. Why couldn't I learn to keep my big trap shut?

At noon Daddy had sent me to the Chicken Roost café next door for French fries and hamburgers and soda pop. We spread out a red-and-white-checked tablecloth and had a picnic in front of the old pot-bellied stove. Daddy told us stories about the early days of the paper, and as usual, Paul asked him a jillion questions. It was like a hundred other Saturdays we had spent together, but none of them had been the last one. We all played like this one wasn't either. Neither of us wanted to leave, but we finally pulled on our coats and started to head out the door.

"Let's get something to eat. I'm starved!" Paul said as the door snapped shut behind us.

"We just ate a couple of hours ago! It's gonna be dark before long. We don't have time to eat. We've gotta find out where John Alan got that Swiss army knife. You're not gonna let a few hunger pangs keep you from taking care of Secret Squadron business, are you?"

"I'm more interested in Swiss cheese than I am Swiss knives," he replied, rubbing his stomach. "No, no! Wait! Make that American cheese! Besides, thousands of people have Swiss army knives. Don't think they have a thing to do with the Swiss army, Rachel. Not anymore, anyway. Switzerland was neutral in World War I, ya know. Heard a guy on the radio say they'll stay out of this one, too. Can't figure how they do that, keep from taking sides like everybody else over there. Most Swiss people speak German, and those who don't, speak French," he finished in that schoolteacher voice he uses sometimes. "They gotta have relatives in France and Germany both, and those countries sure aren't neutral."

"How do you know all that junk?" I demanded to know. "Like Beauregard and the Civil War and what languages they speak in Switzerland? Sometime I think you just make up things because you're a big showoff," I said to be mean, since he wasn't doing what I wanted him to do. If I could get really mad at him, it wouldn't hurt so much to say good-bye. "You're a big Know-It-All!"

"Unlike some people I know, I never make things up," Paul retorted. "I listen to the news every day. And I read. I read all about Switzerland in the 'Weekly Reader' that you hate so much. It's a very interesting newspaper. They've covered a country a week all year. Last week it was Switzerland, Miss Rachel Know Nothing!"

Neither one of us said a word for a whole block. Finally, Paul broke the silence.

"You know you blabbed way too much in front of your father and John Alan, don't you? They'd both come straight to you if Mr. Johnson had any trouble at his Flying Red Horse. Might even decide to check out that outhouse. I'll be gone in a few days, but you're gonna have to live with John Alan for a long time, Rachel."

I didn't say anything back because I was too busy trying not to cry.

"Hey, truce, for today, okay?" Paul said, ruffling my hair. "Let's stop by Carter's and get a cup of hot chocolate with marshmallows and a donut. I'll buy!" Carter's is a Rexall Drug Store, but they have the best soda fountain in town and their hot chocolate is great. I needed something to make me feel better.

We made our way down the Christmas-crowded street to Carter's. Just as we were going in, we met John Alan Feester coming out. His arms were loaded with brightly wrapped Christmas presents.

"Well, we meet again! You two wouldn't be following me, would you? Are you in need of more aid and comfort?" he rattled on as he brushed past us. "I am so glad I was able to aid your father, Rachel," he said, holding the door open and keeping other people from being able to go in. "When you need aid, just call on me. I gladly give aid . . . and comfort, too, any time I have the opportunity," he added, almost doubling over with laughter in spite of the many packages in his arms. The door banged shut behind him, but he stood on the other side and smiled through the glass, bowing up and down until we turned away.

"What was that all about?" I asked Paul as we threaded our way through the jammed aisles toward the booths at the back. We got the last empty one. Neither of us said another word until Elizabeth, Miss Cathcart's younger sister, came and took our order. Jobs at Carter's are usually passed from sister to sister.

"Aid?" we repeated at the same time after she had left.

"Why did John Alan used the word 'aid' four times in ten seconds?" I demanded of Paul. "You heard him. First he said, 'I was glad to *aid* your father. Then he turned right around and said, 'I'll be glad to *aid* you ...' And then he said it again. 'I gladly give *aid* ... and comfort, too.' He said he was gonna 'aid' us at the shop this mornin', too. What does that mean? Nobody talks like that. People talk about first-aid or Band-*Aids* sometimes ..."

"Yeah, like when they are talking about Gypsy Rose Lee's cousin," Paul chimed in, with that silly grin coming over his face again.

"... but I never heard any kid say he'd give 'aid' to somebody. 'Comfort' either, for that matter," I continued, ignoring Paul's dumb interruption.

"But we did *read* those words, and not very long ago either," Paul reminded me. "Remember, we were lookin' up Words of Wisdom? That quote from the Constitution about treason? It said giving 'aid and comfort' to the enemy makes you a traitor to the United States of America."

"But the only reason John Alan Feester would know and use that word on purpose would be if he had been reading the Constitution, too. And the only reason he would check out the Constitution would be if he was spying or doing something else illegal, and he was tryin' to find out what'd happen to him if he got caught! He's a traitor! That proves it! Why else would he use those words, Paul? Tell me that! Where would he have come up with 'aid and comfort'?"

"John Alan is smart, but not that smart, Rachel. There's not a kid alive that smart. He wouldn't think to look in the Constitution to see what happened to traitors before he decided if he wanted to be one. We only stumbled on to that traitor stuff by accident. Where could he have heard about 'aid and comfort' to the enemy?" Paul puckered up his lips like he does when he's in a spelling bee and trying to remember how to spell "lieutenant" or "rendezvous."

"Of course!" he exploded, slapping the table with the palms of both hands so hard the spoons bounced up in the air. "It would never occur to him to read the Constitution, but it would occur to him to eavesdrop outside the window when we were doin' the W.O.W.! It was the one spot we didn't check! Outside the window! He was furious that we got picked! Bet you everything in your Christmas stocking that's what happened! He listened outside the window to see what we were up to. Mr. Snow had to close those windows!"

"But why'd he keep saying 'aid' to us over and over again? What was he tryin' to prove?"

"That was John Alan's way of tellin' us he heard every word we said about him! It was more fun than just flat out admitting he eavesdropped. We're his enemy, and he was able to give us 'aid and comfort' by fixin' your dad's typewriter. He knows we think he's a traitor. Now he thinks the whole thing is a big joke on us. You saw him laughing. If he were a traitor he'd be scared, not amused."

"Then he's not a traitor or even a spy or saboteur?" I moaned. I really wanted to cry now. "I know Captain Midnight is right when he says that there are people like that in the United States, but I guess maybe John Alan isn't one of 'em." That idea was going to take some getting used to.

"To tell you the truth, Rachel, the way you like to make up stories in your head, I think it was more fun for you to think about getting John Alan deported than it was to think about the war. Or it bein' Mr. Snow who smashed the laundry window or Al havin' to go in the army or... or..."

"Or you getting deported to California," I added, looking straight at him for the first time in a long time. "Well, even if John Alan *was* a traitor, with you in California, I'd have to find somebody else to be the second witness anyway."

Witness! That reminded me of what I had been meaning to ask Paul—about the two witnesses he talked about when we were doing the Words of Wisdom, the two witnesses he said could testify against a traitor. But just then Elizabeth arrived with our order and that changed the subject from John Alan back to food.

She had our hot chocolate and donuts on one end of a big tray, and somebody else's hamburgers in baskets filled with hot French fries on the other. The smells from the burgers and fries floated over the booth.

"Hey, Elizabeth, trade ya my donut and chocolate for that burger basket! Even throw in a Joe DiMaggio baseball card," Paul teased. But Elizabeth just gave him a bored, tired look.

She slid our two cups onto the table, plopped the donuts on napkins, and dropped a ticket in front of each of us. Paul reached for mine as she rebalanced the tray on her hip and said, "Pay at the cash register on your way out. We're too busy for me to make change today." She looked like her feet hurt real bad.

I spooned the half-melted marshmallow into my mouth and took a sip of the very hot chocolate. "Don't burn your tongue," I cautioned Paul, pushing John Alan out of my mind. "This stuff is really hot, but it smells so good I can't wait." I put my nose near the rim of the thick ceramic cup and took a deep breath. Then I bit into my donut. It was stale.

"Bet they don't even sell hot chocolate in California. Never gets cold out there," Paul sighed into the gloomy cloud which was now hanging over our booth. He took a big bite of his donut and made a face. It was too late in the day for donuts. "Billy Joe's cousin lives there, and he says in junior high everybody in school has to take ballroom dancing, even the boys! Can you believe that? Ballroom dancing! In school. I'm gonna refuse."

"Oh, Paul, you won't still be living out there by the time we get in junior high," I told him. "That's a whole year and a half away. The war can't last that long. It'll be over, they won't need defense plants anymore, and you'll move right back to Apache, Oklahoma."

"I wish I could believe that," he said, stirring his

chocolate around and around. "It'd make gettin' through Christmas a lot easier. Mom's so sad about leaving, she won't even put up a tree. She already packed our decorations for the move."

I sat and stared at the New Year's poster for 1942 which hung over the pharmacy at the back of the store. It was a carnival scene with Father Time dressed in a long white robe riding on a carousel pony. The New Year's baby was riding on a silver swan in front of him. The baby's diaper was about to fall off. I stirred my chocolate as I looked back and forth between the poster and Paul. Paul's face was as long as the beard on Father Time.

I could tell that neither one of us wanted to go back to the subject of John Alan. What was left to say? He thought we were a couple of twerpy kids, and he was right. Paul never thought John Alan was a traitor to begin with. I made him help me. But Paul was moving, and I'd have to look at John Alan's grinning face and listen to his "aid" talk the rest of my life.

"Hey there, you two, where's your Christmas cheer?" Al's familiar voice sliced through the babble of shoppers who now packed the drug store. "Can my buddy and I join you? This place needs a visit from the fire marshal in charge of crowd control!"

Al slid in beside me and a soldier who was behind

him slipped in next to Paul. It took me a full ten seconds to realize that the soldier was Joe Bob Snow! He looked so different. So much older. I had not seen him since the going away party, but that had only been last June. He looked like a man instead of a friend of Al's. How'd he get old so quick?

"Hey, Rachel," he said with a big grin. "How's fifth grade? Been keepin' this big carrot top out of trouble?"

I have had a crush on Joe Bob for a very long time. I don't even get mad when he calls Al and me carrot top. Joe Bob doesn't treat me like a little kid, and he never teases me like Al's other friends do. He's two years older than Al, but they became good buddies when they were on the junior high basketball team clear back when I was in first grade. Al's always been great at basketball. He was the only seventh-grade kid who got a uniform on the junior high team. He rode the bench that year, but he and Joe Bob practiced together every day, and Joe Bob spent lots of time at our house. Until he left for the army.

"I'm real sorry about you havin' to move, Paul," Al said, reaching across the table to mess up Paul's hair and punch him on the shoulder. "I know what it's like to lose a friend," he added with a nod at Joe Bob.

"Hey, Paul, I understand your old man's gonna go to California to make bombs for me to drop out of my airplane. Tell him thanks for me, okay?"

"Well, I don't know if he's gonna be making bombs," Paul said, shaking his head. "Only thing I know for sure is that we leave January 1."

Somebody dropped a nickel in the jukebox, and "Santa Claus is Coming to Town" filled the air.

"Hey, Elizabeth!" Joe Bob yelled across the din. "How about some service for a serviceman and his friends?" Elizabeth's face lit up in a great big grin as she made her way toward our table. It seemed to me she sure had to wiggle a lot to get there.

"What you need, Soldier Boy?" she said, patting Joe Bob's Army Air Corps patch with her free hand and smiling all over herself. Paul and I didn't get that kind of service. Her feet got well quick.

"Four hamburgers in baskets for me and my friends," Al told her. "You are looking at a very rich man! I just got paid, and I got a Christmas bonus! Mr. Schwartz says I'm the World's Champion Meat Deliverer!"

"How long you get to stay home, Joe Bob?" I asked him, thinking about Mr. Snow. And the flag salute on the playground. And the "yah" brick. I hoped Joe Bob's leave from the army was a long one.

"Got to start back January 1, just like Paul, here," he said with a big smile. "We're both gonna kick off 1942 right by saving the world for democracy!"

"Do you really *like* being in the army?" Paul wanted to know. "All that marching and taking orders. Doesn't sound fun to me."

"It's not supposed to be fun, kid. It's supposed to toughen you up so when you get over there, you'll be ready. Look at this," he said, holding up his arm and flexing his muscles. He was a lot stronger looking than I remembered. I could tell Al was really impressed. So was I.

"Damn it, I wish my folks would sign for me," Al said, shaking his head and pounding his fist on the booth table. I had never heard Al cuss before, and it sounded wicked. And exciting. I started to tell him that I wouldn't tell Mama about him cussin', but then I realized that would be a real dumb baby thing to say. For once I kept my mouth shut.

Elizabeth wiggled her way through the crowd with our drinks and four burger baskets on her biggest tray. She looked like she was dancing.

"Hey, that was quick!" Joe Bob told her. "Crowded as this place is, thought we'd have ta wait a long time. You're gittin' a big tip, Lizzy." He gog-

gled up at her the same way Paul grinned at Gypsy
Rose Lee's picture.

"Mr. White moved your ticket to the top of the
pile when he saw that *you* were in this booth," she
smiled, patting Joe Bob on the arm again. "Told me
not charge you one red cent for Joe Bob's burger,
fries, nor Coke neither. Mr. White wants to buy Joe
Bob's whole meal. Said those who are defending our
country will always eat free at Carter's." She winked
at Joe Bob as she emptied her overflowing tray and
gave Al the ticket for the rest of our order.

Mr. White owns Carter's. He's in a wheelchair
from polio, but that doesn't keep him from being the
jolliest person I've ever known. Daddy told us that
when Mr. White heard about Pearl Harbor, he drove
right down to the draft board the next day and tried
to enlist. He's got a special car with hand-operated
pedals. He told those draft board people he didn't see
how being able to walk or not had anything to do
with being able to fill prescriptions. He told them
President Roosevelt had trouble walking, too, but
that didn't keep him from running this country. But
they turned him down anyway. Daddy said it sure
made Mr. White mad.

"Free food at Carter's! One more good reason to
go dodge bullets!" Al laughed as he punched Joe Bob

on the arm. "What a deal! Better not whip those Germans too quick. Drag it out a few years, and you may get free hamburgers and French fries and Cokes for the rest of your life!"

"Yep..." Joe Bob grinned, taking a big bite of his free hamburger. "For the rest of my life!"

Things got real quiet for a minute after Joe Bob said that. None of us knew exactly why, so we all got busy dipping our French fries into the ketchup and munching on our burgers and sipping our Cokes.

Then somebody dropped a nickel in the jukebox, and the Andrews Sisters singing "The Boogie Woogie Bugle Boy of Company B" reminded us that a war was going on, and we were in it. For the rest of a lot of people's lives.

CHAPTER 20
Good-bye, Paul

Christmas came and went without the usual fanfare. Most people were more interested in listening to the radio and writing letters and sending packages to their relatives who were going in the service than they were in opening presents.

Paul and I tried our best to not think about John Alan or Mr. Snow or even spies and traitors and saboteurs because our time together was getting so short. But that was hard to do since we listened to "Captain Midnight" every day of the week. Once war was declared, the action really heated up, and the Squadron was in even greater danger than ever.

Before we knew it, it was New Year's Eve. Mama

invited Paul's family for supper that last night because she thought Mrs. Griggs would be too tired to cook and not have anything left to cook in, but Mr. Griggs said they had too much left to do. He wouldn't even let Paul come over to our house. To tell the truth, I was glad because I was afraid I would bawl all the way through the meal and make everybody feel even worse.

Mr. Griggs did accept Mama's offer to make a lunch for them to eat on the road to California. She packed a big brown cardboard grocery box to the brim. First, she put in a whole fried chicken with lots of bread and butter sandwiches to go with it, and an ice cream carton full of baked beans. She added a jar of homemade dill pickles, a specialty of hers, and some deviled eggs and carrot and celery sticks. That was dinner. Then she stacked turkey sandwiches on one side and pimento cheese sandwiches on the other. That was supper. Then she tucked apples and oranges in every available spot and covered it all with a brand new dishtowel she had embroidered special for Paul's mama. She stood and looked at the towel for a long time, running her fingers around the edges. Then she went over to the sink.

"That's a redbud tree on the corner, isn't it?" I said, inspecting the white linen cloth more closely.

"The state tree of Oklahoma! We learned that in Oklahoma history. Paul'll like that, too. He loves history. Loves your food, too, Mama." I was getting more miserable by the minute.

"Yes, I thought the redbud would make her think of home," Mama said with a sigh, her voice as lonely as I was feeling. "Don't know if they have them in California. Got redwood, but don't know if they have redbud." She looked down at the soapy water and smiled a really sad smile. "Don't know why, but doin' dishes always makes me homesick for my mama and daddy and our old house in Bishop. I'd wash and Claude and Otis would fight over who got to dry. Wish they were here to fight with each other tonight." She swished her hand around in the water. Mama had her own set of sorrows.

A gold foil-covered candy box with "Pangburn's Chocolates" scripted across it lay on the top of the towel. Daddy had given it to Mama for her birthday last year, and after we ate all the candy, she said the box was so pretty she was going to save it forever. Today I had watched her fill it with pecan and date-filled sugar cookies, Paul's favorite.

By the time Mama had stopped fussing with that box and sat back down at the table, we had finished supper, and the sun had gone down.

"I'll walk ya over to Paul's," Al told me. "I'll carry the food. I'm the 'World Champion Deliverer,' remember? Mr. Schwartz says so. Besides, looks pretty heavy to me," he said, pushing his chair back from the table, but not getting up. In fact nobody seemed to want to be the first to get up tonight. We sat and looked at each other and at the empty fifth chair. When we bought the new round kitchen table last year, Daddy got an extra matching chair because Paul ate with us so often. They had to special order it from St. Louis, and we had Woodward's wait to deliver the set until Paul's chair came in.

"The boy needs his own chair so we don't always have to drag in one of those heavy ones from the dining table," Daddy had said. "And that way he'll know he's family."

We all sat and stared at the food box and didn't say anything.

Finally, Daddy broke the silence. "Those folks'll be eating from that for months after they get to California, Emily. Hope they don't get ptomaine poisoning," he teased, trying to lighten the mood. "You gave 'em enough to last through the spring thaws."

"They don't have thaws in California," Mama reminded him. "Never gets cold enough to freeze out there. They won't make it through Texas if they put this box in the back seat," Mama said, getting a catch in her voice. "You know how Pauly eats!" She hadn't called Paul "Pauly" since first grade, when he announced that he would never again answer to that baby name. Grandpa Griggs had been his only exception.

"It gets plenty cold in Oklahoma, though. You all bundle up good," Mama warned Al and me as she gave the towel a final pat and pushed her chair away from the table. As always, food was the way Mama comforted. I knew the rest of my family was going to miss Paul, too. But not nearly as much as I would.

Al and I trudged down the four long blocks to the Griggs' house. "Step on a crack, break your mother's back," I chanted and looked up to see if Al would object or smile. But instead he said, "If sayin' that makes ya feel better, keep it up, Red. Reminds me of when you were a little kid."

But nothing made me feel good right then, so I sighed and began to scuff my feet along the sidewalk. "Al, when Joe Bob left last June, what'd you say to him while you were waiting at the bus station?"

"Can't remember," Al said, wrinkling up his brow. "But when he left that time, I was pretty sure I'd see 'im again around Christmas. When he leaves next week, it's gonna be harder 'cause nobody knows what's liable to happen since we're at war. War changes all the rules," he finished, kicking a pile of leaves that had blown up near the curb. They swirled up, and then drifted slowly back down onto the cold cement.

"You don't think Joe Bob will die in the war, do you, Al? I'm positive somebody we know couldn't get killed . . . could they?" I didn't wait for him to answer for fear of what he might say. "At least I don't have to worry about Paul getting killed in California. Not unless the Japanese bomb California like they did Pearl Harbor. You don't think California'll get bombed, Al, do you?"

"Na, I don't think California'll get bombed, Red, but to tell you the truth, I am scared for Joe Bob." By this time we were walking up the steps to Paul's little frame house. "You can make it in with these boxes if I balance 'em right. I'll knock for ya and then wait out here by the tree. Don't be long, okay? Hope you and Paul can say good-bye in private. May not be possible, though."

He knocked on the door, and we heard Mr. Griggs bark, "Come on in and close the door behind you fast! It's freezin' in here!"

Al opened the door, I stepped inside, and he pulled it quickly shut behind me. The radio was blaring "Deep in the Heart of Texas," and Mr. Griggs was sitting at the kitchen table drinking a bottle of beer. He was tapping his foot to the music and banging the bottle on the table every time the chorus clapped.

I looked around for Paul, but he wasn't there. There were three small candles scattered around the room, a red one on the kitchen cabinet, a green one on top of the refrigerator, and a taller white one on the table. Each one had a little sprig of holly next to it. That was the only sign that Christmas had come and gone.

"Happy New Year!" Mr. Griggs bellowed without turning around to see who had come in. "That's a fine tune, ain't it? But it ain't *Texas* stars we're gonna be seeing soon. It's *California* stars! And I don't mean them movie kind, neither." He belched loudly and slapped his belly as he turned to look at me. "Want to dance?" It wasn't his first beer.

"Is Paul home?" I asked, taking a step back in the shadows after I had hurriedly slid the boxes onto the table. The towel kept the cookie box from slipping off. I was wishing real hard that Al had come in with me.

"He and his Maw gone over to tell Ruth good-bye," Mr. Griggs told me, looking up with bleary eyes and stroking the stubble of a beard. Ruth Schwartz was Mrs. Griggs' best friend—her only friend, as far as I knew. She lived in the little yellow house just north of Paul's. Her husband ran the meat market where Al worked. They didn't have any kids, so she doted on Paul and was always knitting him mittens and caps and baking him good things to eat.

"You'd think I wuz carryin' 'em off to Timbuktu the way they's all takin' on. Why, we's gonna be richer than Midas 'fore they know it, and neither one of 'em is one bit grateful!" He banged the bottle on the worn yellow oilcloth again just as Paul and his mother crept in the back door. She had a loaf of Mrs. Schwartz's famous rye bread in each hand, and Paul had a stack of mittens and caps in his arms.

"Hey, Rachel," Paul said, rushing forward to see if I needed help. "You okay? How long you been here?" He gave his father a questioning glance.

"Oh, I just walked in," I assured him as I helped him stack the mittens and caps on the table. We carefully sorted them out by size and color. It gave us something to do. There were six matching sets in three different colors and sizes. All of Paul's were red, his favorite. His mama's were white, and Mr. Griggs' were black. "Gee, Mrs. Schwartz must be the world's fastest knitter. The Red Cross is lookin' for people like her," I told him, forcing a big Pepsodent smile. He smiled back and nodded.

"Can't stay long. Al's waiting for me outside

and... and..." The tears I had been holding back were starting to squeeze out the corners of my eyes, so I blinked hard and started talking as fast as I could as I backed toward the front door.

"The Pangburn's box doesn't have chocolates in it, it's cookies," I prattled. "Mama got the chocolates for her birthday, remember? She was savin' that box for somethin' special. Your favorite kind of cookies, Mama says, but she says you always say whatever kind she fixes is your favorite so who knows if that's true, right? It's that recipe she got from Angie Moran. You remember Angie? She always gave us cookies on the way home from school when we were little. She lives in that white house with the green shutters on the corner, the one that always needs painting, but we figured they probably couldn't afford it with Charley being outta work and all..." I was rattling like an Ace of Spades clipped to the spoke of a bicycle wheel.

All the things I had planned to say about how much I was going to miss him were piling up on top of each other inside my head instead of coming out of my mouth. All I really wanted to do was get out of that room so I didn't have to look at Paul and his sad face one more minute. I had been talking so fast that I ran out of breath.

"Well," he said, slowly scuffing the toe of his shoe back and forth on the worn green flowers in the linoleum. "Good-bye, then. Thank your mother for the cookies. They *are* my favorite kind. And thank her for the rest of the food." He nodded toward the boxes. His mother had not said a word. She was looking at the green candle so hard that I thought her stare might put it out. But it didn't.

"Well, good-bye then," I echoed, as I turned to the door. I rotated the handle slowly, remembering how many times over the years I had yanked that beat-up old brass knob open or closed. Until right that minute I never thought about how important that doorknob was. It would open somebody else's door next week. I pulled it shut for the last time and began to cry.

CHAPTER 21
"I'm still here, Red"

"Let's go cry where it's warmer," Al said after a couple of minutes of letting me sob into the front of his wooly warm coat. "I got a key to Pop's office. He won't care if we stop by there on our way home. The walk'll do us good, and we can talk a little bit."

Al always knows just the right thing to do. He took hold of my hand like he used to do when I was a little kid. We haven't held hands in a long time because I thought it made me look like a baby. But tonight it felt really good, even through my mitten and his glove. And besides, it was dark and nobody could see.

The sky was so clear and crisp it looked as if I

could reach up and pluck a silver star off that long strip of dark blue velvet and pin it on my coat. The weather reports had been saying all week how "unseasonably warm" it was for December. Lots of years we have huge snowfalls on Christmas.

"I'm glad it's not sleety and icy like it is most years in December," I said, swinging our arms in rhythm to our steps and trying to pretend this was an ordinary walk on an ordinary night instead of the worst night of my whole life. "Paul's daddy's old Chevy doesn't have a very good heater and one of the windows is cracked." The lump in my throat made it hard to talk.

"I know you're gonna miss him, Red," Al said, giving my hand a squeeze. "The rest of us will, too, you know. Paul's been one of our family ever since he followed you home like a lost puppy when you kids were... what was it, three or four?"

"Three," I said with a gulp. " 'Member how I told people Paul's last name was Dalton like ours? We convinced those dumb Pilkington kids who lived down the street that we were twins but had to live in different houses because Paul was Catholic and I was a Methodist."

"I never heard that one," Al snickered, "but the best, the craziest thing you ever did was when ya tried ta dye his hair red with Mama's liquid shoe polish! Ruined ever one of her best towels. Made a bigger mess than I'd ever come up with, and believe me, I made my share. Pop and I nearly busted a gut laughin'. And lucky for you, Mama thought it was pretty funny, too!"

"What time is it?" I asked to change the subject. All that remembering was making me feel worse.

"Just after seven," Al replied, walking over to the street lamp so he could read the dial. "Hope Pop left the stoves on high enough the place is warm. He usually turns 'em down when he's gonna be gone a day or two. The pot-bellied cools off pretty quick when you quit stokin' the coal in."

He unlocked the door, flipped on the light, and strolled over to Daddy's rolltop desk chair. It was snug and warm inside, so we both took off our coats and piled them on the counter at the front.

"Pop forgot the stoves," Al said. "War's made everybody forgetful, seems to me. Remind me to turn 'em down before we leave. Now, Miss Rachel Elizabeth Dalton," he said in the tone of a lawyer interrogating his star witness, "relate to me in detail the latest misdeeds of the infamous John Alan Feester, Junior, whose only purpose in life is to pester you." He crossed his arms in front of his chest and leaned way back in Daddy's chair. It was the first time he had acted like my crazy big brother since Pearl Harbor. It was good to see him smile. I thought he had forgotten how.

I studied him for a full thirty seconds while I decided whether or not to tell him about me thinking John Alan was a traitor and Mr. Johnson was a spy.

"Do you promise not to laugh if I tell you? Cross your heart and hope to die, promise?" I said, crossing my own heart and spitting in my hand.

"I promise," he answered solemnly, making a big X across his chest and spitting into both palms. "But, first things first. Where do I wipe all this spit?" He grinned.

"Just use your pants. That's what I do," I told him, rubbing my hand up and down on my wool slacks. "This is serious business, Al."

"I can tell. I'm all spit and ears," he said as he wiped his hands on his pants and then cupped both of them around his ears. He flapped them, trying to look like Dumbo the flying elephant in the movie we saw last summer. I cried when I saw that movie, and I felt like crying now.

"W-e-l-l," I said slowly, wanting to be sure I was telling it right. "Captain Midnight says that there are saboteurs, spies, and traitors all around us," I began. "He talks about 'em all the time."

"True, true," Al encouraged me. "Especially now that we are at war."

"I know Captain Midnight is a radio character, but a whole lot of what he says and does is true and real. Did you know that on the Friday before Pearl Harbor was bombed on Sunday, that very Friday, Captain Midnight flew to Hawaii because he thought there was gonna be trouble with the Japanese?"

"Nope," Al said, shaking his head and propping his feet up on Daddy's desk. "Didn't know that. Seems like a very big coincidence."

"It's more than a coincidence, Al, Captain Midnight's friends with people high up in our government. He says even people who look like ordinary citizens and who live in ordinary towns can be spies or saboteurs and cause a lot of trouble for our country. He says there are Americans who might turn traitors if they get the chance."

"That's being written up in the newspaper now," Al agreed. "Pop's startin' to run civil defense columns every week."

"I didn't know that! I hope there's lots about how to catch spies and traitors! Paul says history is full of people who betrayed their own countries. Ordinary people turned traitors. People like Benedict

Arnold. Even George Washington was fooled by Benedict Arnold. You know about Benedict Arnold?"

"Sure. Everybody knows about Benedict Arnold. Worst traitor who ever lived," Al responded, slapping the desk and giving me the courage to go on.

"Well," I took another deep breath, "when Paul told me about Pearl Harbor being bombed, I began to suspect John Alan Feester right away. He fits the description of the bad guys on 'Captain Midnight,' guys like Ivan Shark and his friends... sneaky... evil... wicked. I think John Alan has a criminal mind, Al, like those guys on the FBI Public Enemies list."

I studied Al's face very carefully, looking for any sign of a smile.

"You thought that John Alan Feester, Junior, had something to do with the bombing of Pearl Harbor..." Al mused, with a look that reminded me of Kenneth Stumbling Bear. Stoic. He picked up a pencil from Daddy's desk and rolled it back and forth between his fingers.

"Well, the newsmen all were saying that what happened at Pearl Harbor was a real 'sneak attack,' and sneak attacks are John Alan's specialty. Remember the firecrackers in the bathroom in November? Remember the outhouse in October?

Who knows? Maybe he belongs to a 'Sneak Attack of the Month' club, and Pearl Harbor was their attack for December."

"Hmmmm," Al hummed thoughtfully. "I see. Any hard evidence against this possible traitor? Other than his past record of possible sneak attacks, I mean?"

"No, and that's where the John Alan part gets really bad," I went on, taking a very deep breath to give me courage. "Paul thought my whole idea was pretty crazy, but I talked him into helping me go through John Alan's desk at school to look for evidence."

"You were skating on a patch of thin ice, there, weren't you, Red?" Al said, setting the chair back down on all four legs and sounding just a shade critical. He leaned forward and looked me straight in the eyes. "What if you had been caught going through somebody else's desk?"

"That's the problem. We were caught. Sort of. That sneaky rotten John Alan was eavesdropping outside the window while we were doing it, and he heard every word we said about him. He heard us saying we thought he might be a traitor, and he heard us reading from the Constitution about what happens to people who give 'aid and comfort' to the enemy. We found that goin' through *Familiar Quotations*. And now he is laughing at us and making fun of us because he thinks we are a couple of dumb little kids." By this time I was crying.

"Aw, come on, Red," Al said, patting me on the head and lifting my chin in his hands. "It's not that bad."

"It's pretty bad. And with Paul gone, I'm gonna to have to face John Alan all by myself. If we coulda found out that John Alan was a traitor, we coulda gotten him deported, and I'd be rid of him. But instead it's Paul who's havin' to go away, and I'm left here all by myself. It's just not fair!"

"I'm still here, Red," Al told me with a wink. "I'm not goin' anywhere. Not any time soon, unfortunately," he added with a frown as he patted my head and my hand.

It felt good to be able to tell Al my troubles. I couldn't tell him about Mr. Snow and the brick because I had promised, but I could tell him about B. Arnold Johnson. I was just about to do that when there was a loud tapping on the window that startled us both so much we jumped up at the same time and bumped heads.

"It's a good thing we both got red hair or one of us might get mad," Al said with a laugh. "Who do you suppose that is?" We looked at the front door.

There stood Joe Bob Snow, waving car keys in the air and beckoning wildly. Al unlocked the door and let him in.

"Hey, Buddy," Joe Bob called, dangling the keys in Al's face. "You're not gonna believe this! Look what I got! Was on my way to your house when I saw lights on here. Some breaking news I should know? Hope not. Don't want our last night on the town spoiled." Al and Joe Bob were going to a New Year's dance at the American Legion Hall. I had heard them making plans on the phone.

"Nope," Al told him. "News from the Philippines is worse every hour, but Roosevelt's promisin' to send 'em help. Everybody's afraid it's not gonna get there in time. But that's Dave Obert's problem right now, not yours." Dave was the son of one of Mama and Daddy's best friends, and he was stationed in the Philippines. When his folks heard from Dave, Daddy always put it in his "Where Our Boys Are Now" column in the paper.

"Well," Joe Bob told him, "we're gonna make like Scarlett O'Hara and not think about that until tomorrow." He clapped Al on the back. "You ready to trip the light fantastic? Saw Miss Mae Ella Cathcart peekin' out the front door of the Legion Hall, and I'm certain she was lookin' for me! Bet Elizabeth, her wiggly waitress sister, will be there, too. You can have Elizabeth and I'll take Mae Ella. 'Course, my uniform will make 'em fight over me, but I'll let you have the loser!"

Miss Cathcart and Joe Bob Snow? Why, Miss Cathcart was at least three years older than Joe Bob! She was an old woman. Why would she be looking for him? I'd have to ask Al about that later.

"Let me turn down the stoves for Pop," Al said, heading to the back. "Then we'll need to drop this beautiful young lady off at home."

"Come on, Rachel," Joe Bob said, grabbing my hand, "sit up front with me. I got Uncle Ned's Buick tonight, so we're traveling in style! Aunt Veda and him are in town for the holidays, but they're gonna stay home with Grandpa and Grandma tonight. What luck! And now I'm gettin' to hold hands with a good-lookin' redhead." He squeezed my fingers and smiled down at me. His hands were bigger than Al's, bigger and rougher. "Don't know how I could be so lucky!"

"You're just a lucky guy all the way around," Al told him, switching off the lights as we piled out the door of the shop and into the Buick. It still smelled new. "Free burgers in the basket at Carter's Drug, a shiny Buick at your beck and call, and Miss Mae Ella

Cathcart waitin' for you to dance with her! What more could a guy want? I predict that 1942 is going to be one hell of a year for Joe Bob Snow, PFC, Army Air Corps!"

The car was as warm and toasty as Daddy's shop had been. I wished that Paul's folks had a fancy car to drive to California. They have to stop to put water in the radiator all the time, even when the weather is cold. I wondered what Paul and his mama were doing right now. I scooted a little closer to Joe Bob, not close enough to touch, but closer.

"Tell Mom I'll be home at a reasonable hour," Al said as we pulled in our driveway. "That's what she always says: 'Be home at a reasonable hour.' But my idea of 'reasonable' and her idea of 'reasonable' don't match. Besides, I may not be strong enough to pull this guy out of Mae Ella's arms," he added, punching Joe Bob on the shoulder. "The army's toughened him up!"

I got out, Al moved to the front seat, and they drove off singing "Deep in the Heart of Texas" at the top of their lungs. Since Joe Bob got stationed in San Antonio, it's their favorite song. They sounded like they were having a great time already. Even with the car windows closed I could hear Al clapping as the Buick rounded the corner and passed out of sight.

Paul's daddy had been singing that song, too, when he was banging his beer bottle on the table. Hearing it reminded me all over again how awful I felt in spite of the fact that Joe Bob had called me "a good-lookin' redhead."

I started up the sidewalk toward our front steps and our door with the butterfly knocker. Daddy likes to tell how he nailed that knocker on the door just before he carried Mama over the threshold. He says butterflies, especially yellow butterflies like the one on our door, bring happiness.

I began to wonder if somehow that butterfly had managed to slip free and fly away. It might have taken our happiness with it.

CHAPTER 22
"Twinkle, Twinkle, Little Star"

Mama had forgotten to leave the porch light on, so I had to hold on to the rail as I made my way up the steps. When I reached the door, I felt all around for the butterfly doorknocker. Finding it, I traced its metal wings with my fingertips and willed it to stay right where it was.

The drapes were open, but the only lights in the living room were the ones on the Christmas tree. Mama wasn't in a hurry to take it down this year. Every other Christmas, she and Daddy worried a whole lot about the tree drying out and the hot bulbs catching it on fire. Every year they would remind each other about that awful fire at the Babbs Switch School, the tragic fire that was started by candles on a Christmas tree and killed thirty-six people. But this year, Babbs Switch had not been mentioned. Pearl Harbor had changed that, too.

I stood there peeking into our dark living room and tried very hard not to think about the war or Paul or Joe Bob or John Alan or anything else bad. But it was New Year's Eve and everybody in the world but me was going to dances and laughing and having fun. Even my teacher was dancing tonight, and with Joe Bob, of all people.

I was all alone on the front porch of my house. My best friend was moving away forever, my worst enemy had enough ammunition on me to last him all the way through 1942, and I was a redhead with freckles and bad eyes.

I didn't want to go into the house because I knew Mama and Daddy would be in the kitchen listening to the news about the Philippines. Even though the radio in there is littler, it gets better reception than the great big Motorola in the living room. The base Dave Obert flew out of was about to fall to the Japanese, and when Mama wasn't on the telephone talking to Dave's mama, she and Daddy had been huddled around that little white radio. This was the first year I could remember when they didn't go to the New Year's Eve party at the American Legion Hut, but Mama said she didn't see how anybody could feel like dancing when a war was going on.

It wasn't very cold outside, so I sat on the steps and looked up at the sky. One star was much brighter than the rest. I tried to think "Twinkle, twinkle, little star...," so I might get a wish, but the star I was staring at changed into Paul's face and crowded the twinkles out of my mind. He was looking out the back window of their old Chevy, and waving good-bye.

I concentrated and changed that back window of Paul's car to a porthole in a big ocean liner. And John Alan Feester was the one waving good-bye because he was being deported to China. Mr. Sing had helped me trap him, and he had talked some of his relatives into putting John Alan to work in their rice paddies so he wouldn't starve. I could hear the whistle on the boat tooting and the crowd chanting "Yah! Yah! Yah!" and I waved and waved until the ship and John Alan were tiny specks in my mind.

Paul says the stories I make up in my head are kind of like the pictures he draws in the dust. I could always tell him my stories, and he could always show me his pictures, and we both knew what the other one was trying to say. I was sure gonna miss that.

CHAPTER 23
A Big, Fat Enigma

"I found that on the back porch when I let Sally Cat out," Mama said when I walked into the kitchen for breakfast New Year's morning. She pointed to a great big box sitting on a chair that had been moved from the table to the corner near the back door. Our kitchen table is round, but everybody always sits at the same spot on the circle. I got a big lump in my throat when I realized that Daddy had moved Paul's chair to the corner and then scooted the other four chairs around the table so the vacant spot wouldn't look so empty. Mama saw me staring at it, and she looked away real quick. For the first time in weeks, the radio was not on.

"Whoever left it must have gotten up before the

sun 'cause it was still dark when Sally Cat woke me howling to get out," she chattered as she opened the oven door. The smell of hot biscuits filled the kitchen.

The package was as big as the dictionary box where Paul and I had hidden John Alan's lunch basket. Remembering that made me wonder how far down the road Paul's car was by now. The lump in my throat got bigger.

"Must be a New Year's present for you, Rachel," Daddy said, taking a sip of his coffee and smiling at me. "Why don't you open it and satisfy our curiosity?"

"Me? If you think it's a present, what makes you think it's for me?" I asked, walking over to get a closer look.

"Because it's got your very clever initials on the top," Mama laughed. She swears that when she named me Rachel for one grandmother and Elizabeth for the other it never entered her mind that our last name, Dalton, would create a lifetime problem for me and my red hair. Sure enough, there were my initials—R.E.D.—printed in red crayon on a piece of white construction paper glued to the top of the box. The writing looked vaguely familiar, but with printing it's hard to tell.

"Whatever it is, it's not nearly as heavy as it looks," Daddy said, filling his plate with bacon and eggs as I started to open the box. "Doesn't weigh much more than one of these prize-winning biscuits of your mother's," he added, picking one up and reaching for the butter. Mama's biscuits have won the blue ribbon at the Caddo County Fair in Anadarko the past four years. She gets her name in *The Anadarko Daily News* every time.

"Wonder who it's from?" I said, ripping my initials from the top. I pulled up the lid and found about a hundred pages of newspapers all crumpled up. "I don't think it's a present at all. I think it's a joke," I said as I rummaged through the pages, getting newsprint all over my hands. "Smells like a John Alan Feester, Junior, trick to me."

Maybe this package would prove that even if John Alan were not a traitor or a saboteur, he was a mean kid. He knew Paul was moving on New Year's Day, and he was making that day even worse for me by leaving me an empty box and putting my initials on it to make me think it was a present. Another sneak attack.

Then, my fingers touched something hard, something hard and smooth and long. Before I even pulled it out, I knew that it was my pencil box.

"That rotten, thieving John Alan!" I exclaimed, clutching it with both hands. "I knew he stole my pencil box! I just knew it! What do you suppose made him give it back today?"

"Is there a note?" Mama asked, looking over my shoulder. "A card or something? You don't *know* it's from John Alan, do you?"

"I know. I know, all right. John Alan Feester is a thief. He stole my pencil box, and now for some unknown reason he's giving it back. Maybe he made a New Year's resolution to reform."

"I wonder," Daddy mused as I rummaged around in the box of paper looking for a note. "Did the unknown person or persons who took John Alan's lunch basket think they were stealing it?"

"What?" I said, halting my search and looking up at him.

"I just said I wondered if John Alan thought that his lunch basket had been stolen by a thief?" Daddy repeated. "*Thief* is a strong word, Rachel. Words are like water dropped on a sandy beach, you know. Once they're out of your mouth, you can't pick 'em up again no matter how hard you try."

And for the first time since he said it, I remembered that John Alan had hollered, "My lunch basket! Some thief stole my lunch basket!"

"No," I said firmly. "Thieves did not steal his lunch basket. Somebody hid it for a joke." I could see that both of them were eyeing me closely. "At least I think that's what happened," I added quickly, and I immediately buried my head in the box again. When my hand reached the bottom, my fingers closed around something warm and fuzzy. I pulled it up. It was a red mitten, one of the red mittens Mrs. Schwartz had knitted for Paul.

"What in the world?" Mama said. "A great big box like that for a pencil box and a mitten?"

"Mrs. Schwartz knitted it for Paul," I said as if that explained everything. I felt around in the box again. More mittens, and caps, too.

Finally, my fingers felt an envelope. I pulled it out slowly. There was no writing on it, but when I ripped it open, I found a letter, a long letter written in Paul's very familiar handwriting on sheets from a Big Chief tablet. Mama and Daddy looked at each other and then at me, but didn't say anything. They acted as if nothing unusual had happened and went back to eating breakfast. The room seemed real quiet without the radio blaring.

I slid the box onto the floor, sat down on Paul's chair, and began to read:

Dear Rachel,
  I don't know how to say this other than to just come right out with it.

John Alan did not take your pencil box.

I did.

I don't know why I took it for sure, but one reason was that I never had a grandmother to give me anything. Another reason was that it was the prettiest shade of blue I had ever seen. Another reason was the two little dog erasers. You know how I've always wanted a dog, and Pop won't let me have one. I know those dogs weren't real, but I pretended they were. Pretty silly, huh?

There is another thing you need to know.

John Alan Feester saw me take the pencil box. So did Kenneth. When I slipped it out of your desk and stuck it in my pants pocket, I looked up and saw John Alan staring straight at me. He didn't smile. He didn't frown. He just looked at me. Then when I slipped it out of my pocket and into my desk to hide it until I could take it home, I saw Kenneth watching me. He never changed expressions. Neither one of them ever mentioned it to me or to anybody else as far as I know. I never have figured out why.

Because John Alan was giving you so much trouble, I knew you would think he had taken it, so in my mind I pretended that he had too. Kind of like when you make up your stories in your head. Your imagination can play funny tricks, you know?

When you and I read in the Constitution about traitors and "the testimony of two wit-

217

nesses to the same overt act...," I knew I was in bad trouble. Not even Captain Midnight could save me, because there were two witnesses who could testify against me, John Alan and Kenneth. They had both seen my "overt act." But instead of being a traitor to my country, I had become a traitor to you, my very best friend. Don't know which is worse.

When I found out I was having to move to California, I decided I was really being deported because I was a traitor and that's what happens to traitors. That's kind of crazy, isn't it? But it's the way I feel.

I hope this won't keep you from writing to me, because I am going to miss you something awful. You and Kenneth both. I'm even going to miss John Alan Feester. You can see now why I think he's not all bad. I'll send you my address as soon as I have one, but it may take a while.

I hope you don't mind that I kept one of the erasers. I only wish it could erase what I did.

Paul

On a separate piece of paper were three post-scripts.

P.S. You can show my letter to John Alan if you want to. Even though he gave me "aid and comfort" by not telling you about the pencil box, that didn't make him a traitor like me. I'm the Benedict Arnold. Showing him my letter might even get him to stop trying to "aid" you, at least until the war is over. What do you think?

P.S.S. This great big box was the only one we had left after we packed. Pop made me stuff all the leftover paper in it. I needed something to put the caps and sweaters in. Also this big box reminded me of the dictionaries. Just looking at it made me laugh. I thought it might make you laugh, too. We've done lots of crazy things, haven't we, Rachel? Remember the red shoe polish?

P.S.S.S. I hope you can read this O.K. The only light I had was a candle. It took me almost all night to write it because I kept tearing up the paper and starting over again. I'm sorry about that, too, because I know that with a war on, we need to save paper. Pop said there was no room for Mrs. Schwartz's mittens and caps and that nobody needed them in California anyway, so take them to the Red Cross, O.K.? But don't tell Mrs. Schwartz. It would hurt her feelings. I know that even *girls* can keep secrets, yah?"

I read the letter twice before I folded it up and put it back in the envelope. Paul had taken my pencil box. Not John Alan. And John Alan had known but not told me. It was going to take a lot of thinking to sort all of this out. But with Paul gone, I had lots and lots of time to think.

Mama and Daddy were both looking at me with question marks all over their faces. I had told them about the missing pencil box, but after the lunch basket incident, I didn't mention it again for fear Mama would ask a lot of questions. Someday I may let them read Paul's letter and tell them the whole story, but not now. They both consider letters very personal, so I know that they won't ask me to let them read it.

"Well," Daddy said after a long pause, "seems we have a bit of an enigma here, so that'll be your word for today—*enigma*. It's a word Winston Churchill made popular not long ago. Want to look it up, Punkin?"

I pulled the dictionary out from between the toaster and the breadbox. We are the only family I know who keeps a dictionary in the kitchen. "Food for thought," Daddy says when people ask why it's there, but it's really because we do my word-for-the-day at breakfast.

"'Enigma,'" I read aloud. "'A riddle; a puzzling problem.'" That was certainly a good word for this day, maybe a good word for the whole new year.

"I remember that Churchill speech, the one where he called Russia an enigma," Mama said, nibbling on a piece of bacon. "It was in the paper about a hundred times. Old Winny called Russia 'a riddle wrapped in a mystery inside an enigma.' That's about as puzzling as you can get."

"Speaking of Churchill," Daddy said as he started to dry the dishes, "did you read what he told that smarty pants reporter at the news conference with Roosevelt last week? I quoted him in my editorial the next day, but I know you sometimes fail to read my wise words since they're not in *Familiar Quotations* yet. Hand me that paper, and I'll read it to you."

Mama retrieved the paper from the pile we were now saving for the war effort. We take them to school every Monday and the teacher measures each person's stack with a ruler. The kid with the highest stack wins a prize. We're starting to save everything for the war effort now, even grease and the tinfoil off our chewing gum (although I haven't figured out yet what they're going to do with any of it).

"This wet-behind-the-ears kid asked Sir Winston to tell him just exactly how long this war was going to last. As if Churchill, or anybody else for that matter, could answer a question like that. Old Winny champed down on his cigar and replied, 'If we manage it well, it will only take half as long as if we manage it badly.' How's that for a great reply? There's not a soul alive who could say how long this or any other war will last. That's the grim fact about war."

We all sat and looked at each other for a minute, and then we all three found ourselves looking at Al's empty chair. He didn't get in until the middle of the night from the New Year's Eve party, so Mama was letting him sleep late. She hadn't even complained to Daddy like she usually did. But his empty chair reminded us that if the war lasted long enough, we might be looking at it and wondering if Al was getting enough to eat. We would never move Al's chair out of the circle. Not ever.

"Well," Mama said with a sigh, "we can only hope and pray that we can heed Churchill's advice and 'manage it well,' can't we?"

There was another long silence.

"You can turn the radio back on now," Mama said to Daddy. She turned back to me. "Daddy and I made a New Year's resolution that at least while we were eating, we'd try real hard to smile and laugh and pay attention to each other just so we won't forget how."

Daddy gave her a kiss and started to turn the radio back on, but he stopped with his hand on the dial. "Speaking of enigmas, Sam Sing brought me back the money that I had collected for his new window. Said he wanted me to give it to the Red Cross. When I protested, he said something that didn't make any sense at all, something about his heart and red peppers. But he seemed so bent on my taking it back, I finally agreed. Then when I passed his shop the next day, I saw Sam and Mr. Snow putting a new glass in the window. I didn't know they were friends, but they were talking and laughing like a couple of old army buddies at a reunion. Now that's an enigma, don't you think?"

I just looked at Daddy and smiled. I couldn't admit that I knew the answer to the Sam Sing/Sam Snow enigma. The dictionary says an enigma is a riddle or a puzzling problem. That word describes John Alan Feester perfectly. He's a big, fat enigma. And my New Year's resolution for 1942 is to solve him.

HOW COULD WE FORGET?

"WHO WON GRANDPA?"

The Way It Was

During the 1940s, people depended on radio, newspapers, and magazines for their news and entertainment. The Sunday "funny papers" were eagerly anticipated, and cartoon characters often became beloved members of the family. Dick Tracy and Tess, Dagwood and Blondie, Little Orphan Annie and her dog Sandy were all considered personal friends.

Political cartoons were on the opinion page, a page reserved for adult readership, but many kids thought the cartoons were meant for their eyes, too. After all, most of these cartoons made their parents laugh, and the kids wanted in on the fun. As World War II dragged on and on, the political cartoons were often anything but funny, but in their own special way they reflected the tone of the times and made people think.

Jim Lange's political cartoons have appeared in *The Daily Oklahoman* for fifty years. When Molly Levite Griffis was doing historical research for this book, she recalled two of Mr. Lange's Pearl Harbor cartoons which had made a lasting impression on her. Oklahoma Publishing Company granted permission to reproduce them here.

Acknowledgments
and Commentary

The birth of Rachel Elizabeth Dalton was attended by a number of midwives and midhusbands, all professionals in their fields. These professions range from newspaper persons to writer to kid (being a professional kid is no easy task) to Sister (if you've never known a professional sister, you haven't met Georgann Levite Vineyard) to librarian, teacher, principal, and friend (professional friends are the ones who love you even when you're bad).

In the newspaper category I had assistance from the crème de la crème: Margaret Taylor, the first woman president of the Oklahoma Press Association; Jane Bryant; Ed Montgomery; Bob Lee; and Bob Peterson. They took turns telling me how small-town newspapers were really put together in the "good old days" of Royal typewriters and printer's ink.

Since I am internet illiterate, the information desk staff of the Norman Public Library used their wonderful skills to answer such penetrating questions as "How do you spell the name of Buster Brown's dog?" (Tige, remember?) or "When did Crayola start making boxes of 64?" Call Marilyn Halvorsen, Patty Wallace, Ruth David,

Linda Jordan, Judy Day, or Chad Fate to find out the answer to that one! They know it all!

Speaking of computers, although this is my fourth book, it is the first done on the "bane of my existence." David Todd, whose patience exceeds that of Job, and Richard Bedard, my in-house tornado expert, spent endless time and energy teaching me how to make a glorified typewriter out of my Gateway 2000. There are still times when entire paragraphs are underlined or in italics (sometimes both), but because Pat Smith and Linda Horton could make my mouse sit up and beg, I was able to send Virginia at Eakin Press a sloppy disk this time. (I know, I know! But *mine* are sloppy!) Marilyn Todd, Dave's wife and my dear friend, read the original version of this book fifteen years ago (this baby had a really l-o-n-g gestation period!) and gave me great guidance.

Kay Austin, Kate Davis, Ann DeFrange, Charlene Dickenson, Karen Johnson, Ruby Soutiere, Jill Weigle, Kaye and Fred Blaylock, Dennis and Billie Letts, Leta and Mike Wimmer have all worn many hats over the years, but if I could buy them new ones at the State Fair of Oklahoma, I'd buy those cute white sailor jobs with red stitching on the brim, the ones that read "Best Friends." Do they still sell those?

Jamie Raab and Elaine Markson, friends of a friend of mine, did more than they could ever imagine to give Rachel the makeover she needed after so many years as a pre-teen, and Anna Myers restyled her red hair!

The readers I love most, of course, are the kids because they are the reason for the writing: Sage Brown, Abby Busking, Katie and Erica Korhonen, Katie Wear, and Tom Menzie's fifth-grade class at Harry S. Truman

Elementary School in Norman, Oklahoma, who read the book in draft form, drank their Ovaltine, and helped create the glossary for this book. And most important of all, my own kids, George and Ginger Griffis, who grew up in spite of all the books I put on and in their heads.

And last, but certainly not least, thanks to the guy who was kind enough to support my move to "The Cave" by becoming a storekeeper. You know who you are.

Glossary

American Legion Hall—building where veterans and others hold meetings.

Baer, Buddy and Joe Lewis—famous heavyweight prize-fighters.

Benny, Jack—early day radio comedian.

blunder—stupid mistake.

castor oil—oily medicine thought to be a cure-all.

central—early-day telephone operator.

Churchill, Winston—Prime Minister of England during World War II.

clapboard house—house made of rough, unfinished-looking wood.

constituents—a group of supporters.

cyclone—terrible wind storm or tornado.

deport—to order out of the country.

DiMaggio, Joe—great center fielder for the New York Yankees.

eavesdrop—listen secretly to someone.

engrossed—giving complete attention to.

expel—drive or force out.

filling station—business which sells gasoline.

Franklin, Benjamin—American patriot in American Revolution.

Gee! Haw!—commands given to mules; gee for left, haw for right.

Hitler, Adolph—German dictator in World War II.

Holmes, Sherlock—famous fictional detective.

hook, line, and sinker—to believe totally, without questioning facts.

icebox—cabinet which held ice for keeping food cold.

in cahoots—cooperating with in a secret way.

incriminating—fact or evidence which would prove one guilty.

interrogating—asking many questions in search for the truth.

Lee, Gypsy Rose—carnival dancer who used fans to cover herself in her act.

lei—wreath of flowers or paper worn around the neck.

linoleum—hard, washable floor covering.

meat market—store which specializes in fresh meat.

Morrow, Edward R.—famous radio newsman.

Mrs. Stewart's Bluing—blue liquid used to whiten clothes.

Mussolini, Benito—Italian dictator in World War II.

nemesis—worst enemy.

O'Hara, Scarlett—heroine in *Gone with the Wind.*

oilcloth—material made waterproof with oil or paint.

ornery—mean or ugly acting.

outhouse—outdoor toilet in a small house with a seat over a deep pit.

phonograph—record player.

pot-bellied stove—warming stove with bulging sides which burned coal.

privy—outhouse.

ptomaine (silent *p*)—sickness caused by eating spoiled food.

Rogers, Roy and Trigger—famous cowboy movie star and his horse.

Rogers, Will—Oklahoma's most famous comedian and writer.

Ross, Betsy—woman credited with sewing the first American flag.

saboteurs—enemy agents sent to destroy defenses and steal secret plans.

scalawag—rascal, scamp, someone up to no good.

stoic—person who shows little or no emotion

Timbuktu—town in west Africa.

transom—small window directly over door or window.

"trip the light fantastic"—dance.

twerpy—ridiculous, unimportant.

USS *Oklahoma*—The battleship named for Oklahoma; sunk during attack on Pearl Harbor, but because news of the American losses was considered a military secret, the fact was not confirmed for some time.

whoppers—enormous lies.

yellow—cowardly action.

Resources

Bartlett's Familiar Quotations. 16th Edition. Little Brown & Co., 1992.

Colman, Penny. *Rosie the Riveter*. Crown Pub., 1998.

Kallis, Jr., Stephen A. *Radio's Captain Midnight: The Wartime Biography*. McFarland and Co., 2000.

Osborne, Mary Pope. *My Secret War: The World War II Diary of Madeline Beck*. Scholastic, Inc., 2000.

Osborne, Richard E. *World War II Sites in the United States: A Tour Guide & Directory*. Riebel-Rouge, Pub., 1997.

Shepherd, Jean. *A Christmas Story*. This movie delights both kids and adults.

To order a replica of the Captain Midnight Code-O-Graph badge call 1-800-558-8944 for a Klutz Catalogue.

To order pocket-size editions of "The Declaration of Independence and the Constitution of the United States of America" for $1.00 each, call 1-800-767-1241.